To Dad, Mom, Nick, and Ethan:

Dad, thank you for all the encouragement, for all the jokes—for everything! Because of you, I wanted this series to take place in Wilsonville, and I'm sure glad it does.

Mom, you're wonderful, and I appreciate your dedication to my series. Thank you for always reading my books before publication and giving me feedback! I love it!

Nick, I know you're so busy with your college; sometimes, they really lay it on thick! Yet, you still edited this book. What a trooper! And... concerning the pork rinds, thank you for forgiving me.

Ethan, whoo hoo! You did it—you read the second book in my series! Looks like you've got a couple more to get through now, but I really appreciate you reading my stuff, and also all the good times.

TABLE OF CONTENTS

Part of a Mystery

Chapter 1

The last leaves had fallen off the trees, bare branches pointing up toward the cold sky. It was 2006 and early January. For a while yet, the season would be chilly. In contrast to the dormant winter, someone full of life ran, bubbling over with joy.

"Race you home!" the person shouted with his teenage voice.

"Out in the snow?" yelled another teenager—this time a girl. "We're going to slip!"

The voices belonged to my two best friends, Kodiak Nobleman and Felicia Blackwood—Cody and Fay for short.

Fay had a point, but I adjusted my leather bag

1

securely over my shoulder and sprinted down the sidewalk.

"It's *on,* Cody!"

Felicia was left behind somewhat in despair without her friends but let out a slight laugh and then hurried off after us, though running a little more carefully than Cody and I were.

I inhaled the frosty winter air deeply and pushed off with my legs as hard as I could.

Cody snickered and looked over his shoulder at me with a grin. His nose was slightly pink from the cold.

Fay was still far behind. Due to the snow, she had enough sense to be more cautious.

Cody suddenly jumped as he ran and then, thankfully, landed with ease. Next, he knelt and dug his hands into the cold powder, playfully molding it into a big snowball.

"Take that!" He threw it at me.

"Hey!" I yelled, as the ball unfortunately collided with my forehead, nearly knocking my gray beanie off. I didn't actually mind, though. After all, I had known Cody my entire life and had gotten hit with more than a few snowballs throughout our friendship.

If anyone loves snow, it's Kodiak.

As we ran, the beautiful ranch where Cody lived came into view.

I sprinted with my whole strength and was gaining on him quite successfully. He just reached

the backdoor before I did.

We stood there, gasping for breath as we waited for Felicia, whom we saw coming toward us in the distance.

Cody grinned. "You almost won, Lydia. Good job!"

"Well, you stopped when you made that snowball; that bought me some time."

Even when I got hit with his snowball, I didn't stop but ran harder.

Fay came up to us in a couple of minutes, and Cody flung open the backdoor, shouting out, "Mom!" while stomping off the snow from his shoes before coming in.

"Cody!" I heard Mrs. Nobleman call from the kitchen. "Don't fling the door so hard, remember? You're going to end up denting the wall again."

I couldn't tell if my friend's cheeks were pink from cold or embarrassment—probably both.

"You're right. Sorry, Mom."

She shook her head with a slight laugh. "I've got stuff for hot cocoa set out; you guys help yourself."

We thanked Mrs. Nobleman.

The three of us marched to the Noblemans' closet to put away our coats and hats and mittens and scarfs—the full load.

Cody looked at Felicia with a smile. "Cold, Fay? Knowing you, I bet you don't even want to put your coat up."

Felicia was always cold in the winter no matter

how many layers she wore, it seemed.

She laughed. "I guess you're right."

"Well, I know how to cure you!" Cody chirped. "Ryker and I have invented the most amazing hot chocolate ever. Come on, I'll show you guys—or *girls,* I guess I should say."

Fay and I watched amusingly as Cody grabbed a big mug with a picture of a corgi on it and dumped way too much hot cocoa powder in. He must have filled it a third full at least. Next, he poured in some hot milk and small marshmallows, stirred it (but not too much, because he loved some of the hot chocolate powder to stay on top), sprayed on a bunch of whipped cream, and then stabbed a candy cane in the side.

"Delicious!" he exclaimed, taking a big gulp. "Want me to make you some?"

My friend Felicia was very polite and ladylike, but even she was tempted and succumbed. "Sure!"

Everyone loves hot chocolate, of course. I heartily agreed to have some as well, and Cody got right to work, grabbing Fay a mug with a pink rose painted on it and getting me one with a beautiful ocean. I loved the sea; after all, my father had been a manager of three aquariums before he died.

My parents, Seth and Liliana Arlington, had been killed—murdered—when I, Lydia Arlington, was nine. Now, I was fourteen—fourteen, and still thinking of them each day.

But when I was with my friends, everything felt

4

good; I was happy.

The three of us headed toward the living room with our warm beverages, and as we did so, Kodiak snuck his hand in the cookie jar, pulling out his favorite snack—a snickerdoodle. He actually pulled out three, giving one to each of us.

We all sat down on the couch, and Cody got out a disc so we could watch a movie on his television set. As he did so, his older brother, Ryker, who was eighteen, came thumping down the stairs.

The two siblings didn't bear a strong family resemblance, with Ryker having dark-brown hair and blue eyes and Cody having strawberry-blond hair and hazel eyes. However, both teens had freckles, and they both had the same nose and grin—a type of grin that was always contagious to everyone around them.

"Hey, Cross Eyes! Hi, girls! What's up?"

The boys both had silly nicknames for each other, Ryker calling Kodiak "Cross Eyes," and Kodiak calling Ryker "Pitchfork."

"We just raided the kitchen and started a fire in the fireplace and are about to watch a movie," Cody explained. "Want to join us?"

"Sure—just let me first loot the kitchen myself."

He went to go do that while the three of us chatted. We made room for Ryker as he came in with a snickerdoodle and a hot chocolate as unhealthy but delicious as what Cody made for us. The four of us, rather cramped, were careful not to bump into

5

anyone.

Ryker took off his reading glasses and set them on the table. It was his senior year of high school, and he was always pretty busy keeping up with his homework. At the start of the school year, he started having trouble reading up close and now occasionally wore some eyewear to help out. Cody said it made Ryker look quite sophisticated.

A grin tugged at the corners of Cody's mouth. "How was the government homework?"

Ryker, rubbing the bridge of his nose, replied, "Pretty good, I guess. Just going over the judicial branch in more detail."

Felicia perked up, always interested in school even if we were only eighth-graders and wouldn't be studying government for a long time. She began to ask some questions, only for Cody to hush her.

"The movie's starting—quiet down!"

She did. However, Cody wasn't always the best at following his own rules as he started cracking jokes and imitating characters. Soon, Ryker was doing the same, so I couldn't help but slightly snicker at the boys. Half the fun of watching anything with them was listening to their own silly commentary rather than just paying attention to the actual show.

Everything felt perfectly comforting. The Nobleman ranch had such a pleasant feeling about it in the winter, with the snow falling softly out the windows and the fire crackling cheerily; the light

from the antler chandeliers bouncing onto the yellow, butter-colored walls; and the big cowhide rug in the center. In our hands were the hot mugs. The warmth seemed to penetrate deeper than just into my hands, as it seemed to make me feel warm and relaxed all over.

With Ryker and Kodiak's rascally ramblings and my own daydreams, Felicia was really the only one even paying attention to the movie. But eventually, the brothers quieted down, and I began to snap out of my reflections on the home.

The film was of the mystery genre, and so I'm afraid to say that with me not paying enough attention at the beginning, I now couldn't follow the plot well.

"Wait, since that jewelry was in the mother's purse, is she being framed?" I asked. "Or did she do it?"

"She *is* wearing glasses, so obviously she's framed," said Cody, cackling at his joke. The boy then grabbed Ryker's reading eyewear off the table. "Pitchfork, did *you* do it? *You're* not wearing glasses."

"Cross Eyes, I believe *you've* got them! Clearly *you're* the guilty one."

The two teens started joking loudly again, while Felicia and I tried to focus on the show.

"Hmm," Fay said in reply to me, her eyes never leaving the screen, "likely a red herring. You never know, it could be that she purchased the same *type* of

7

stringed pearls."

Ever attentive, it seemed, Felicia loved anything that caused her to think. She was always at the top of her class and was prone to get rather depressed when the school year ended. Of course, she also was human and loved summer vacation, but her craving for knowledge was admirable.

Cody, on the other hand, would gladly do anything to extend his summer break. He *did* enjoy school, but try as he might, things always went in and out of his head at a surprisingly high speed. The strawberry-blond teen was improving, though, getting better at applying himself.

Before long, the movie's credits were rolling.

Felicia sighed. "As focused as I was, I still didn't catch that surprising twist at the end. Who would have thought the captain's son was behind it all the whole time. And he seemed so close to the protagonist!"

I reminded myself to pay closer attention next time.

After a little more time spent with the Noblemans, Felicia and I realized how we'd be heading home in the dark if we didn't leave quickly. Ryker and Cody offered to accompany us back, and we consented to their kindness.

Bundling up, we headed into the snowy scene.

"Oh, Fay, by the way," I said as we walked, "see you tomorrow for our sleepover. We're still on for it, right?"

"Of course! I wouldn't miss it for the world."

"Me neither! Maybe we can watch another mystery movie."

She agreed, saying that would be very enjoyable. As a house came into view, I concisely replied, "All right, goodbye."

But I wouldn't have imagined that starting the next day, I'd be part of a different mystery myself.

Unsolved for Six Years

Chapter 2

A few days, weeks, or months, and you're fine. Then the next day, you just wake up staring at the ceiling and wondering when the pain will be completely behind you. You wonder if it will *ever* be gone.

One of the hardest yet most powerful lessons to learn is acceptance. Some things are out of your control, but certainly not all. Acceptance is learning to let go of the past. Letting go isn't becoming calloused or insensitive; in fact, a part of letting go is

grief. Really, bottling up pain just makes it worse because when you're brimming full of sorrow, it becomes impossible to constrain it. Eventually, it *will* explode, which is definitely *not* what you want to happen. One shouldn't lash out at another, so pain must be released appropriately.

As years went on in my own experience, and I began to learn to live without my father and mother, I would sometimes have a memory without feeling gloom, but rather *gladness*. Acceptance doesn't hold you back; it just heals your heart.

That being said, a part of you will always miss your loved ones, but you learn to be at peace with yourself. You find joy in life again. It's a learning process, and though I was getting better, I was still trying to deal with it and failed at times.

"Good morning, Grandmother," I called out as I entered the kitchen.

My grandma was busy cutting some peaches. "Good morning! Would you stir the oatmeal, Lydia? I think it's about to scorch!"

I went to do as asked, the steam floating up and warming my face. Something about oatmeal on a chilly day was always comforting.

"I was going to take Charity and go to the bus after breakfast. Is that all right, or do you need me here for a while?"

Charity was a little dog with black, brown, and white spots that my parents had given me before they passed away.

"I don't mind when you go, so long as you're back in time to help straighten things up before Felicia comes over," she replied with a smirk.

I agreed.

A few years ago, I had stumbled upon the strangest thing—an abandoned bus filled with books in a deserted alleyway. Later, I found out my secret wasn't originally *my* discovery but that my own *mother* had found the bus as a girl. Something about going there always seemed to calm me.

How the bus even got there in the first place is an interesting thing too, but in short, it was stolen some years back.

Anyway, after some time, I had let my grandmother and friends in on the secret of the abandoned bus—but no one else. It was our own special place.

Excited for some time at the bus, I prepared to hurry off as soon as breakfast was finished and the dishes were cleared.

Tying my deep-brown hair into a braid and tossing it over my shoulder, I then threw on my dark-violet coat. As I put Charity's blue and orange collar on her and attached the leash, I called out a goodbye to my grandma and set out.

The buckles on my boots clicked merrily as I walked down the sidewalks. Some time passed and then, turning a corner into the alley, I slowed.

As always, the bus was there, filled inside with books. My intention today was to try organizing the

12

volumes within, at least to some extent.

Perhaps I could make it a little easier to walk around inside. Even with me occasionally stacking books in an orderly fashion, I had never sorted and organized them all. Furthermore, due to frequent visits from that of my friends and me, even the books that *were* sorted got into a mess before long. But the heaps didn't bother me much; they just gave it a more mystifying and wild feeling.

Charity lay down outside near the bus steps while I picked up a few volumes. I had to be careful not to get too sidetracked looking *inside* the books, but rather to stay focused on putting them away in proper order.

Still, my mind wandered to the stories within.

I attempted to organize them by category but ended up having trouble with certain books that overlapped into multiple genres.

While tiring a bit mentally from my concentration and work, my eyes wandered toward the front of the bus, where the bus driver would have once operated the vehicle.

For a moment, I felt swept into the past, imagining young children coming inside and sitting down, talking, staring out the window… It must have been so long ago.

I moved toward the front and looked down at the steering wheel. My hand rested on it.

After a brief moment of silence, I turned around to resume my work. However, I then stopped short,

suddenly remembering something so long ago, it felt like a dream.

I had a strange recollection from a few years prior. I was in my old house—the one I lived in with my parents—doing homework at the table. While studying, I heard my father and mother upstairs. It couldn't have been more than a few weeks before they died. The conversation had sounded strange, even though I only heard bits and pieces because I was busy studying. It was just now that a phrase spoken so long ago returned into my mind, and what an obscure string of words it was!

The chair seven seats back.

Hadn't that been what Father said?

What could he have meant? I failed to recall any more of their conversation, yet those five words drew me in, enticing me.

"Seven seats back..." I murmured. A bus had enough seats to go back that far and more. Could he have been talking about the bus?

Slowly, I walked down the aisle until I reached the seventh row. My eyes scanned over the chairs. I began to grab some of the books on the seats and move them out of the way.

Nothing.

"What could he have meant," I wondered aloud.

Maybe I needed to look more carefully at the books I had grabbed? Scanning each book, I didn't see anything particularly fascinating.

What if the conversation I had heard from my

parents wasn't anything more than just small talk? Did it even contain any significance?

I dropped to my knees and looked under the seats on my left. But upon finding nothing there but some dust, I turned to the ones on my right.

Sharply, I gasped. There *was* something underneath the chair by the window.

Reaching, I pulled out an object which apparently was abandoned for some time but in good shape, nonetheless. My hands shook.

A small, brown book. I recognized it from my father's office in Scottsbluff, at the aquarium he once managed. Upon skimming the first few pages, I found out it contained small notes, a few sketches, and things about the sea creatures he watched over.

Why did he put this here?

Then, as I was turning through the pages, my eyes fell on something that made my heart skip a beat.

In my father's recognizable cursive, I saw a single sentence on an otherwise blank page. To myself, I quietly read the words aloud: "What really happened on October twenty-first, 1999?"

* * *

Not more than half an hour later, I was back home, helping straighten up things for when Felicia would be over that night. As I worked, however, all I could think about was the book I had found, which had been tucked away in my leather bag with a turquoise-colored flap. I had slipped the bag into my

closet when I returned and was now left thinking about the secret.

"Grandmother?" I asked.

"Yes, Lydia?"

"I have a bit of an odd question."

My grandma laughed. "Okay, try me."

"Do… you remember anything significant about October of 1999?"

Grandmother knit her brow. "That *is* an odd question!" It only took her a moment's reflection until she then said, "Why yes, I do remember something—oh… it was just dreadful."

My hands stilled while putting a book on a shelf. "What do you remember?"

"Well…" she said with a sad sigh, "a young woman died in Scottsbluff that month—"

"*What?*" I gasped. "Was it a murder?"

"I don't think the cause of death was ever revealed. But this is what was really odd—she was a worker at the aquarium in Scottsbluff."

I briefly pondered that statement for a moment. It felt vaguely familiar that when I was little, I heard of an aquarium worker's passing, but the years and the obscurity of it all made it fade like a dream. I don't think I had been told much about the death at the time.

"My parents died at the Ashland aquarium… Grandmother, three aquarium worker deaths less than two years apart? Doesn't something feel off about that?"

16

She nodded. "It was something I never really could understand. But I guess over time, I realized maybe there were some things I wouldn't get answers to, and even if I did, it wouldn't bring me my daughter, son-in-law, or anyone else back."

Tears glistened in her eyes.

"Still," I said, "didn't you feel a deep desire for justice?"

"I did. But as the years went by, I guess I just lost hope."

We were silent for a moment, until I said slowly, "What do you know about the death in 1999?"

She paused for a moment, recollecting her memories from six years prior. "I believe she was only in her early twenties. The woman worked as a receptionist, and that's about all I remember. But what brought this up, anyway?"

"Hang on," I said, running to grab the journal I took from under the chair seven seats back.

"It's almost a repeat from when I discovered Mother's diary in the bus a couple of years ago, but I found this book of Father's in there."

Handing it to her, I said, "I'd recognize Dad's writing anywhere."

She flipped through the pages, and I directed her to the one with the intriguing phrase on it.

Father had known something. But how? And what? What mystery had he been striving to uncover shortly before his *own* death?

As she looked at it in silence, I stated, "There

was more to the story. There had to be!"

What happened that day from six years ago? I had no idea, but I was determined to find out.

* * *

Felicia was here for the sleepover, and I couldn't help but show her the secret that was hidden in the bus.

"So," she began, handing me back the book, "the death was likely never solved. But Mr. Arlington definitely must have known something."

Fay bit her lip in thought, sitting on my bed with one leg crossed over the other. "Shouldn't we tell Cody?"

I nodded. We were going to see him tomorrow anyway; it would be Sunday.

"Yeah, after church," I responded, gazing at Father's journal in my lap as I sat on the floor. Then I looked up abruptly. "We have to finish what he started. Or... at least I have to."

Fay's eyes widened and she opened her mouth to speak, but then she closed it. The teen then reached for the book.

While flipping through the pages, Felicia said, "Maybe there's some type of clue around here."

A period of silence ensued.

She looked up and squinted a bit in thought.

"Some of these notes don't make sense; they are so random and abrupt," she said, motioning to the pages.

"That's what I was thinking."

18

Felicia tilted her head in thought. "I believe there's something important here if we can just decipher the phrases. I think... I think I want to help solve this."

I half smiled at my best friend. "It's all just like two years ago, isn't it?"

She smiled back. "Indeed. We just need Kodiak, and then we'll be all set."

And so that's just what happened. The next day, after worship services, I thanked the preacher for another edifying and scripture-filled sermon, and then I greeted the brethren, conversing a bit. Walking out of the church building's backdoor afterward, I scanned with my eyes to find my friends. Cody and Fay were standing by a large tree near the front doors. Quickening my pace, I gave a wave as my eyes met Kodiak's.

"Hey, Lia!" he chirped.

"Hey," I replied. "Cody, you're never going to guess what happened to me yesterday."

He cocked his head to the side, his hazel eyes big and full of questions.

Voiced lowered, I filled him in on everything as quickly as I could before my grandmother would come out ready to leave.

The strawberry-blond boy's jaw dropped in astonishment.

To conclude, I added, "I have this feeling Father was so close to finishing what he started but never got the chance. I want to finish it."

"And," Fay piped up, "so do I. So, are you with us, Kodiak?"

He looked from me to Felicia. An expression of determination shined in his eyes. "Am I with you guys? Of *course.*"

Warmth for my friends washed over me. Not more than a few seconds later, I saw Grandmother walking out of the building.

"I've got to go," I said. "But let's talk soon. Thank you so much, both of you!" And I followed my grandmother into her glossy, red convertible, waving to my friends as we drove off.

* * *

For six years, the mystery of the woman in Scottsbluff had been unresolved. I knew that her passing must have left hearts broken, dreams crushed, and memories tainted bittersweet. Her loved ones needed closure, and for the mystery of my own family, I did, too.

So a plan was in action.

It was Monday. Cody, Fay, and I were walking through the school hallways.

"I was looking into stuff," Felicia began. "My father keeps old newspapers in a stash from time to time, and we had one from the month of November in 1999. He usually keeps papers with any extremely surprising story on them, and never have I been so relieved he does!"

Cody was struggling to get his locker open, brow furrowed. The locker was finicky, tending to get

20

jammed more often than not.

"What did the paper say?" Kodiak asked, jarring the dial.

"A receptionist named Liesel Allen was found at the Scottsbluff Aquatic Museum in the morning on October twenty-first, 1999. The cause of death was unknown, as she had some health problems even though she was only twenty-three, but authorities were looking into the case. It doesn't look like they ever solved it, though," Fay said with a sigh.

One of our older friends, Justice Gravett, came to help Cody with the locker. Like Ryker, he also was a senior, and a good friend to Kodiak. (Since Cody's best friends—namely, Felicia and I—are girls, he especially appreciates having a guy to hang out with at times.)

"You've got to get used to this thing soon enough; you had the same problem with your locker *last* year, Cody," Justice chuckled. He hadn't heard our current conversation, or else he wouldn't have been so jovial.

"Thanks for the help," Cody replied with a slight laugh. "For some reason, I always get paired with the worst lockers!"

We went to school in Beaver City, Nebraska, and the school covered seventh grade up to twelfth.

Justice nodded in understanding. "I think you'll get the hang of it. Just push in almost like you could bust it open, but don't *actually* break it. Oh, is it so late already? Sorry to cut things short, I'd better

21

make it to my class."

With that said, he waved goodbye after managing to open the troublesome locker. Turning around, Justice walked to his class with a brown-haired girl, Amity. She was his twin sister and best friend. She waved to us as Justice had done and smiled sweetly.

After they disappeared among the other students, I turned back to face my own best friends.

"So... Liesel Allen was her name?" I asked, bringing up our previous conversation. "Guys, ever since last month, Grandmother has been planning to take me to the Scottsbluff Aquarium this Saturday. So maybe while I'm there, I can look for information?"

Cody stuffed a book into his backpack and then shut the sneaky locker. "That'd be a good idea. Plus, maybe we can find some stuff out before then, too!"

Fay nodded. "I'm in favor of that. But for now, we'd better get going before we're late for our *own* class."

She was right. With a slight sprint, my friends and I dashed off.

SUSPECTS

Chapter 3

The rest of the week went by slowly. My father's journal gave us a vague idea of what might have been intended, but my friends and I couldn't know for sure. It had been Father's private book, after all, and was apparently written in a way that only he could decipher—which perhaps would have been a good thing if it had happened to fall in the wrong hands.

Unfortunately, my friends and I weren't able to find out any extra information before Saturday. In fact, other than seeing Cody and Fay each day at school and at church that Wednesday, I hadn't spent

any other time with them. Grandmother and I had a vigorous amount of "winter cleaning" that week, Cody had been busy helping around at his family's ranch, and Felicia had tons of choir practice, so none of us had time.

Fay and Ryker were in choir together—Felicia a soprano and Rhys a tenor—and much to everyone's dismay, this was their last year together, with Ryker being a senior and all. But for their upcoming choir event, the two each had soloist lead parts for the same song, which they were thrilled about. It would certainly be fun when all of us went to their event!

Needless to say, the two were frequently trying to memorize songs and practice singing the notes right.

As the week approached and Saturday rolled around, I grew restless, trying to practice patience. I hadn't mentioned anything more to my grandmother about the journal or death in 1999, but it was always in my thoughts. After the rather long drive, we pulled into Scottsbluff Aquatic Museum. My heart thumped as I swung my brown leather bag—which had a turquoise flap and contained the journal, among other things—over my shoulder.

Since my parents' passing, numerous times I had been to all the aquariums my father once managed. But this time, I looked at the large structure in a new light.

What were you trying to tell the world, Father? What secrets did you know inside the book?

Holding the door open for Grandmother, I gazed into the building as if I were a statue.

After my father's death almost five years ago, the new manager of the aquarium told me I could go anywhere in the aquatic museum I wished, whenever I desired. He still worked there and was happy to see me.

"Oh, Lydia! How are you?"

I shook myself a bit to loosen up and then entered with a small smile. "I'm quite well, Mr. Colville, thank you. How are you?"

Hezekiah Colville was a very kind man of about fifty. As a boy of nineteen, he had left his family and friends in Virginia to pursue schooling in Pennsylvania. He then migrated to Illinois, Arizona, Florida, and finally, Nebraska, where he had remained the past fifteen years. All of his children were grown and married, scattered throughout the state so that only he and his wife were still in Scottsbluff.

"I'm well, though always busy it seems! Might I help you with anything?" he asked.

"Yes, actually," I said, looking toward my grandmother. She nodded, permitting me to wander around the building. I then turned back to the manager, saying, "Would it be okay if I could enter

the filing room?"

"Sure, what's ours is yours. I'll take you there."

Turning to Grandmother, I told her to go on without me and that I would meet up with her soon. She agreed and headed off in the other direction as I followed Mr. Colville.

Recalling how my father would have once gone down these same hallways, a feeling of longing washed over me as I walked. Although I was the only Arlington of my immediate family left, I felt like my parents were almost with me again as I recalled memories of the three of us here on relaxing trips. But really, I was still just alone. Blinking back a few tears, I stifled a sigh.

Mr. Colville and I approached the door, which had a plaque that said in bold words:

FILING ROOM. STAFF ACCESS ONLY.

An employee was nearby in the hall but nodded to Hezekiah, not offended at his bringing a visitor in. He was the manager, after all. He could basically do whatever he wanted.

Unlocking the door, Mr. Colville pushed it open and let me inside. Another man was within the filing room, doing some work at a desk. He looked a bit younger than Hezekiah, maybe around forty. The person glanced up at our arrival and then rose. I'd

seen him before, though I'd never met him personally. He was the assistant manager.

"Hello, Zeb."

"Hello, Mr. Colville—and…?"

"This is Lydia Arlington; she's the daughter of our late friend and previous manager, Seth."

"Oh—right," Zeb said quickly. He then held out a hand for me to shake. "Zeb Bayer. Nice to meet you, miss. I'm very sorry about your parents."

I slightly smiled in appreciation. "Thank you."

Looking at both of us, Zeb said, "Did you guys need me to get you something?"

"I'm all right; thank you, though," I said. "I was just going to look around a little on my own."

Zeb gave a single nod and then set back to his work.

Not wanting to waste time, I quickly made my way to the files, eying the rows which were sorted by year and month.

Giving me seclusion to look on my own, Mr. Colville worked with some papers on a clipboard in his hand.

There, I thought, finding the folders labeled for October of 1999.

There was a list of all the workers as well as their schedules. It contained any sick days and vacations for the month.

With a little digging, I found Liesel Allen's

records.

Apparently, she had two sick days that month, on the tenth and the eleventh. She also usually got off work at noon, working part-time.

Quickly pulling out a plain, purple notebook from my bag, I wrote down this information.

In the records, I found a couple of workers that had leave on the twenty-first, the day Liesel died. If Liesel had been *murdered,* it would be less likely for them to be guilty, since they probably wouldn't have been there.

I looked for the names of those who had any shifts that day. As fast as I could, I recorded the people's names. Of course, it wasn't even certain if anyone had played a role in Liesel's death, but the information could very well come in handy.

As I looked for more clues, my heart skipped a beat and I held my breath after finding the records of my own father. There wasn't a whole lot logged on each person, but I quickly wrote as much as seemed necessary in my notebook.

Medical records were highly confidential, so I couldn't get any employee information on that.

Then, I stuffed my notebook back into my bag, placed the original papers back in the folder, and stuffed the packet into its proper shelf. I rose quickly, not wanting to draw attention to myself by looking at the files for a long time.

Returning, I headed over to Mr. Colville, and he glanced up from his clipboard.

"Ready to go?" he asked.

I smiled. "Yes, thank you for taking your time to help me."

"Always at your service," Hezekiah Colville replied, leading me out of the room.

* * *

The next day, we were at the Blackwoods', for dinner.

After supper, Kodiak, Felicia, and I headed upstairs. Ryker remained to converse with Miles Carpenter, Mr. Blackwood's intern who had just turned twenty-two, as well as to be with the adults for a while. Fay's little sister, Leanne, remained downstairs too, of course. Upon arriving in Felicia's room, I tossed my bag onto her pink bed and pulled out my father's journal as well as my notebook.

We all sat down on the floor in a circle.

"So," Cody asked, his forehead creasing in question, "what did you discover yesterday?"

"I found the records from the month and year of Liesel Allen's passing and wrote down each worker that was present that day, as well as brief information about them."

"Good thinking, Lydia," said Felicia with an encouraging smile.

Turning in my notebook to the page with the

names, I showed my friends. The list ran thus:

Liesel Allen
Seth Arlington
Zeb Bayer
Hezekiah Colville
Blaire Forbes
Ava Taylor
Trace Turner
Edith Webb

"Of course," I began, "this is just a list of the workers for that day; it doesn't mean any of them *did* it. For example, we already know my father wasn't guilty—if anything, he seemed to be trying to solve the case—and Liesel Allen was the victim. It's also possible that she did die through other causes, like health problems."

Fay nodded in understanding. "There are a lot of factors."

"But," added Cody, "this is a good start!"

Grabbing the notebook and looking through the list, Felicia said, "So who still works at the aquarium?"

"All of them except Edith Webb, Blaire Forbes, and… my father of course."

Fay gave me a sympathetic smile. "Did any documents say why Miss Webb and Miss Forbes

left?"

"I found, through some quick searching in a file from 2002, that Edith moved to Beaver City, actually. As for Blaire, I couldn't discover anything and was running out of time."

Cody's eyebrows shot up. "You know what that means, right? Quick, Fay, grab the phone book— we've got to find Edith!"

Anxious to retrieve evidence, Felicia darted out of the room. After running inside her father's home office, she soon returned with a large book, and she hastily turned through it to get to the "W" column.

No one under the name of Edith Webb appeared.

"What?" Felicia exclaimed in despair. "She has to be there!"

"Do you have any older phone books, Fay?" Cody asked, trying to console her. "Maybe she got married and goes by a new last name. If so, we can find her in an older book that would still have her old name."

"We don't have any except for this year," the teen replied, running her hand through her sandy curls. Then, with a slight laugh, she added, "We only keep old *newspapers,* not phone books."

Kodiak took ahold of the phone book. "Well, assuming she still lives in Beaver City, we'll find her eventually if we search long enough."

He then tediously skimmed the pages for Edith.

"Here's one," he said. "Edith Sandusky. Here's the info for her; I guess you'd better record it, Lia, and then I'll keep looking."

There could be multiple Ediths, after all.

After a long while of some more searching, Cody found two more candidates: "Edith McKenzie" and "Edith Levy."

After I recorded the names down, I sighed. We couldn't even be sure if any of these were *the* Edith we were looking for.

"Shall I call them?" asked Fay.

I nodded, thanking her.

We followed Felicia to her home phone, where she carefully dialed for Edith Sandusky.

It rang once, then twice, and before long went into voicemail. Fay, who hadn't planned for that, hung up.

"I'll just try the second one," she said, flushed a little from embarrassment.

Dialing and then double-checking to make sure she got the numbers right, Felicia pressed the button to call.

A moment later, Cody and I faintly heard a woman's voice say, "Hello?"

"Oh, *hello!*" Felicia breathed. "I hope I've reached the right person; I'm looking for a woman by the maiden name of Edith Webb?"

I held my breath.

Fay beamed, saying to the person on the line, "That's you? Oh, wonderful! Is it okay if I ask you a couple of questions—oh, forgive me, wait! My name is Felicia Blackwood. Well, actually, would I be able to schedule a time to talk with you about the Scottsbluff Aquatic Museum?"

Fay continued talking for a few minutes, grabbed a piece of paper, frantically wrote some things down, and then hung up.

Cody looked at her inquisitively, and Felicia grinned at the two of us. "I'm *so* glad! Mrs. McKenzie was very sweet, and she has arranged for us to talk with her tomorrow at her house in Beaver City."

Kodiak and I both looked at her beaming face in astonishment. "Fay!" we exclaimed, bewildered.

I stammered a bit. "What, Fay—how are we going? We can't—"

"—can't what?"

We turned to the voice and saw Ryker, who was confused and amused by our conversation. "What's going on?"

Then Cody beamed as much as Fay had before. "Pitchfork! Will you *please* take us after school tomorrow?"

"Take you guys where, Cross Eyes?" he inquired.

"To Edith McKenzie's!"

"Edith who? Cody, do you have a girlfriend you didn't tell me about or something?"

Cody flushed. "No! Mrs. McKenzie is a *married* woman," he exclaimed, quite offended, "and most likely over *twice* my age."

"Well excuse *me,*" Ryker said with a mischievous smirk. "I had no idea. Are you smitten with her daughter, then?"

"I don't even know if she so much as has one," the strawberry-blond boy replied in a huff, shaking his fist angrily. "Now pay attention, you old rascal."

We quickly filled Ryker in on the *real* reason we wanted to go to Mrs. McKenzie's house, and his eyes went wide.

"That's crazy," he breathed, surprised but also appearing quite interested.

I looked up at him, my eyes pleading a bit. "Will you take us then, Rhys?"

"Well…" he hesitated. After a moment, he smiled a little bit. "Okay… sure, meet me outside after school, and I'll pick you three up."

We thanked him again and again, which caused him to laugh a bit and blush, saying it was nothing.

"I'm happy to help, really."

I smiled at my friends. We actually were getting somewhere, weren't we? We were going to solve this mystery one step at a time.

* * *

34

The next day, after school, we piled into Ryker's truck, with Cody sitting in the passenger seat and Fay and me in the back. Cody instantly turned on the radio, goofing off with the different stations.

"Requests, ladies?" he asked with a smirk, turning around in his chair to see Felicia and me.

"I vote oldies," I replied with a laugh.

Felicia giggled as well. "Classical, please."

"Come *on,* Fay," Cody pleaded, "pick something good. Why not some Spanish music, you giggling schoolgirls?"

"I *did* pick something good, you goose," Felicia somewhat retorted.

"Señoritas?" Ryker asked with a large grin. "How about some oldies and classical songs on the way home, and the Spanish station right now, just for kicks?"

Felicia and I agreed.

"Code?" I questioned, amused. "Why did you request this station—can you even speak Spanish?"

"No," he replied. "But it's still fun; it reminds me of going to a Mexican restaurant!"

"Yeah," Ryker said as he pulled out of the school, "and of *you* eating too spicy of a pepper."

"I *love* spicy food," Cody replied in defense. "You're the one who had to ask for bread to ease the heat."

"That was just *one time,* Cross Eyes. I've built up

a tolerance ever since."

The siblings got into a mild (no pun intended) sibling quarrel over who could handle spice more, which was more of a joke than anything else, but they settled down as we approached the McKenzie house.

"Besides," Kodiak quickly added, "Felicia can't speak Spanish, and she's listening to Mexican music."

"Well, I didn't request the Spanish station, Kodiak. You did."

Cody ignored her response. "Say, Pitchfork, is there a French station?"

Felicia's mother had moved from Paris to America as a little girl.

"I don't know," Ryker replied. "But we're at our destination anyway."

We walked in file up the driveway and to the front door.

Upon arriving, Ryker rang the doorbell, and silence ensued for a brief moment.

There were two long, thin windows covered with sheer curtains on each side of the door. One of the corners of the left curtain swayed to the side toward the end, and I thought I saw someone peek through.

Then the knob turned, and a woman who appeared to be in her early thirties with long, flowy black hair opened the door, carrying a baby. A young

boy was standing near her to her left. Most likely, he had been the peeking figure I saw.

"Hello!" we called out.

Fay stepped forward and extended a hand. "I'm Felicia Blackwood, the one on the phone yesterday. Your children are so cute! What are their names?"

The woman smiled. Motioning to her sons, she said, "This little one is Liam—he's about eight months, now—and this is my four-year-old, Aiken."

We introduced ourselves in turn.

"Won't you come in?" Mrs. McKenzie asked.

Entering the house, we thanked her as she led us to the living room. The place was very polished, but also homey. Everything seemed scrubbed and glowing, while the walls were decorated elegantly with sweet family pictures and things. The fireplace mantle had a bouquet of fresh roses even though it was January.

"Make yourselves at home, please. There now, how may I help you guys? You're wanting to know about the Scottsbluff Aquatic Museum, right?"

"Well, yes, to an extent," I responded. "You see, ma'am, my father was Seth Arlington, the previous manager of the place. I've been going there off and on my whole life, but lately, I've been trying to find information on something."

She nodded with a soft smile. "I remember Mr. Arlington—he was a fine man, and I'm sorry for

"Yes, I haven't heard from her in a long while. She quit working at the aquarium and moved back to Omaha rapidly after. It's no wonder! Finding one of your own friends gone at your workplace... I did hear that in the fall, she got engaged, so I imagine she's healing slowly."

Mrs. McKenzie was caught up in past recollections for a moment. "Anyway, what got you interested in Liesel?"

"Various things," I replied vaguely, not wanting to go into much detail with someone I barely knew. Just because Edith didn't mind talking about what she knew didn't mean I felt like doing the same myself. "Mrs. McKenzie? Was Ava Taylor a friend of Liesel's?"

"*Oh,* Ava! She worked the shift after Liesel and is one of my close friends still."

"Auntie Ava?" asked a young voice, and we saw Aiken peeking out of his room's doorway.

Edith smiled. "Yes, Auntie Ava! We'll be done soon, dear."

"Sorry for interrupting, Mama," replied the little boy, and he went back into his room.

Felicia smiled a little, saying, "My little sister is a bit younger than your son, ma'am. She's three."

Mrs. McKenzie thought that was very sweet and started talking about little children. Fay, who loved babies and small kids, couldn't resist, and soon Edith

was letting Felicia hold baby Liam. The teen laughed gleefully but then became a bit more somber, saying, "Anyway, we don't want to take up too much of your time. I think we just have one more question."

Fay shot a quick look at Ryker, Cody, and me as if to confirm. I gave a slight nod.

Felicia turned back to Mrs. McKenzie. "Were any of you guys friends with Trace Turner?"

"Oh, Mr. Turner! He's still working over there and is best friends with Zeb Bayer. Trace and Ava met at work when she applied and got hired. They're engaged now," she explained with a look of fondness in her eyes.

"That's so sweet," responded Fay, and Kodiak gave her a look that seemed to imply he thought she was silly. He playfully rolled his eyes, but I thought that deep down, he believed it was sweet too.

"Thank you for taking your time to speak with us, Mrs. McKenzie," Ryker said, standing up. "I think we'd better be going now, but we really appreciate it."

Cody, Fay, and I agreed.

Edith smiled and went to open the door for us. "It was nice to meet you guys."

She talked to us briefly for a bit longer, then we left.

Once we got into the truck and Ryker started the engine, he furrowed his eyebrow a little dubiously.

"Mrs. McKenzie is pretty friendly, but I'm surprised she told so much to four teens she doesn't even know."

I nodded at his fair point. Pulling out my notebook, I recorded all the information Edith had given.

As Ryker pulled out of the neighborhood, Felicia said, "We learned a lot, but I would have thought she'd be a bit more discreet."

"At least it worked out in our favor," Cody added with a laugh, reaching to turn on the radio.

A Walk Through the Woods

Chapter 4

The rest of the week followed. I went to school, spent time with my friends, and did all the other things I usually did. Unfortunately, I tried to work more on the mystery but to no avail.

It was Thursday. Walking toward the shelves in the school library, my eyes skimmed through the books. Since study hall was almost over, I needed to put something back onto the shelf for earth science. Fay, Cody, and I had been doing a project for oceanography this week. To be honest, I enjoyed

earth science—more than I thought I would—though not as much as Felicia. And I was especially glad I got to work with my friends.

Finding the empty slot on the shelf, I was just about to put the book away and turn to go when I stopped.

"Never say that again!"

The voice came from the aisle on the other side of the shelf. Looking through the gap in the bookshelf where the hardcover was supposed to go, I peered at the sight. The scene surprised me.

A tall, blond boy, no doubt a senior, was smirking with his arms crossed at another boy, an eighth-grader with dark-brown hair. I recognized the younger teen at once because he was Trevin Aragon, Cody's bully. The seniors and eighth-graders had the same study hall time.

Trevin was scowling at the blond boy, indignant, but the other just seemed amused.

"I'll say it again," the senior said, his voice almost a whisper in the quiet library.

Trevin clenched his fists, eyes icy.

Though he was mean, Trevin wasn't your average bully. While tall for his age, he was still quite a bit shorter than most of the guys at the school, considering he was only an eighth-grader. Thin, not particularly muscular, and apparently happiest when studying, Trevin didn't seem like the bullying type. In short, however, he didn't pick on people with his *fists,* but rather with his *words,*

which still hurt.

Now, he was in front of a young man that was a head taller than him, well built, and seemed to be in quite a disagreeable mood.

Regaining my composure, I felt a need to try coming to Trevin's defense, even though I didn't like his general manner. For some reason, I was sorry for him. Yes, he was a jerk and a bully, but he still was a human being and a fellow eighth-grader. And eighth-graders didn't stand much of a chance against high schoolers, at least the older ones, anyway.

However, just as I was about to pull myself from my place, the senior opened his mouth to speak. But suddenly, someone cut him off.

"Honestly, Bastian? Leave the kid alone."

I was even more surprised when I realized the person coming to Trevin's aid was one of my friends—Ryker Nobleman.

"I'm just talking to him, so what?" the young man apparently named Bastian, retorted.

"I'd daresay you're doing more than just conversing about the weather."

"Look, if you want to intervene in my discussions, we can take this outside after school, okay?"

But I thought that even as Bastian said such, he was trying to put on a brave face he didn't really have.

Ryker half smiled. "I don't think either of us wants to do that. Let's just end this and leave it

behind."

"You're just scared."

"Maybe a little," Rhys replied calmly. "But I can tell you are too."

Just as Bastian was about to snap a sentence out, the bell rang sharply. Ryker tilted his head toward the exit as if beckoning Bastian to leave, so the senior rolled his eyes and left.

"What was Bastian giving you trouble over?" Ryker asked.

Trevin dropped to his knees and gathered up his books. "He was talking bad about my… my…" The boy's eyes flashed, anger bubbling up inside. "He was telling lies about my father."

The older boy looked confused. Ryker Nobleman was one of the nicest teens in the school, and everyone knew it. He didn't mind stepping up for the younger students, who couldn't as easily defend themselves. Not surprisingly, Ryker was held in such esteem by nearly everyone there that even Trevin, who couldn't stand Cody, liked him. If necessary, he didn't mind confiding in Rhys.

"My family's, you know, kind of financially unstable. Bastian was talking bad about Dad because my older brother has to work as well to bring in the funds for everyone. And I've got to do the same thing in a year or so."

Ryker nodded. "I see. Well, don't let Bastian get to you. There's nothing wrong with needing to work. He's just jealous of you or something, most likely."

46

"Jealous of me?" Trevin asked, looking a little unsure. "I don't see why anyone would be jealous of me."

"Well, you're pretty smart, and he's… well… not as much."

I wondered how Trevin couldn't feel guilty over the way he treated Cody. Maybe sometimes, he did.

Leaving the room, Trevin gave a slight wave goodbye to the other teen. A moment later, Ryker was about to exit as well. I shoved the book I had borrowed back into its slot.

"Rhys!" I shouted, sprinting a bit to catch up with him.

Upon seeing me, he raised his eyebrows and put a finger to his lips.

"Shh," he whispered. "Libraries and study halls are supposed to be quiet, remember, Lia?"

We turned out of the room.

"Oh," I said, a bit embarrassed. "Does it really matter? I thought it would be okay with the bell having rung and all."

He grinned. "Maybe. But we'd both better be getting to our classes."

Ryker walked with me to my class, as mine was on the way to his, and then waved goodbye. While the teacher was closing the door, I sank into my chair right next to Fay, just in time.

Felicia leaned sideways toward me, whispering, "Bring your father's journal tomorrow. I want to see if we can find anything else out."

I nodded. She, Cody, and I were going to hang out at the bus the following day.

Cody, who was sitting a row in front of us and a few seats over to my left, turned to give me a look that said, "Where were you?"

I, in turn, sent an expression that replied, "I'll explain later," giving a sideways smile to my strawberry-blond best friend.

Smiling back, he turned away.

* * *

My friends and I were poring over the journal with extreme intensity.

We were inside the bus because it was bitterly cold out today. The shelter helped, though Felicia was still shivering in her pale-pink wool coat. Cody had even lent her his mittens.

The three of us were currently looking at a map of the aquarium that had been drawn with careful detail by my father. We then read the phrase on the next page beside it.

"What does he mean?" Cody asked, tilting his head a bit. "It just says, 'North, then southeast?' and goes on without mentioning anything else."

"Father had his own style of notetaking," I said. "But unfortunately, I think he was the only one who could understand it. He always just wrote down bits and pieces."

"Even so," replied Fay, "it must be referring to the map in some form, right?"

"I think so."

The map was labeled with all the places and rooms in the aquarium, such as the area with the whales and other large marine life, the reef tunnel, the water quality lab, the jellyfish room, the staff offices, the filing room, the meeting room, the breakroom, and even my father's own manager's office, among other locations.

The areas farthest north included the area with whales and other large creatures, the backdoor, the water quality lab, and the resource room. When Father said, "North, then southeast," he could have been referring first to any of these, I supposed, or possibly even the jellyfish room, which was below the water quality lab; or the reef tunnel, which was below the resource room.

Then, southeast would contain an area of most of the small marine life, a second resource room, the staff offices, the breakroom, the meeting room, Father's office, and maybe the filing room and janitor closet.

Directly south was the main entrance and admission.

"Well," Felicia began, "I'd say as far as by 'north' he meant either the water quality lab, the jellyfish room, or the backdoor, as the other areas are more northwest and northeast."

I carefully wrote those three places down as candidates in my own notebook.

"And," Cody piped up, "by 'southeast' he most likely meant either the meeting room, the manager's

office, or the breakroom, but you could put the staff office and the filing room down as unlikely possibilities."

I did so. "But still," I said, "we don't know the significance of this."

Felicia shrugged. "Yes, but it's a clue, and that itself is important."

"Wait," Kodiak began. "Something doesn't make sense. You can't really *go* north and then southeast at the aquarium. If you started north, you would have to go south to get to the door that leads to the other rooms we mentioned. There is the area with the small sea creatures where you could walk directly from north to southeast, but that area isn't really on the southeast *side* of the map unless you go as far east as you can."

Fay nodded in thought. "It could be that he meant to go to the small marine life area, then?"

"Maybe," I agreed, "but I don't know for sure. Oh, how I wish Father had just said who went *where!*"

Shrugging, Felicia said, "We don't really know what it means. Perhaps even *he* didn't know where they went."

Cody looked at her, exasperated. "Then why *write* anything?"

I thought I understood what Fay meant. "Wait," I said. "He could have just been giving a hypothetical, right? Maybe a suspect could have gone *from* somewhere north and ended up at a place on the

southeast side. We have to look at it in steps."

If we didn't get stuck in the details of one phrase, maybe that would make it easier. I looked at a second quote, written a little lower on the paper. "Hmm, Dad said, 'She could have gone to file.' That's odd. I wonder who 'she' refers to."

Taking my own notebook, Cody flipped back to the page where I had recorded the list of people who worked for the aquarium in 1999 on October twenty-first.

"Well, 'she' must refer to either Ava Taylor, Liesel Allen, Edith Webb—now Edith McKenzie— or Blaire Forbes."

I handed Cody my pencil, and he wrote the names, as well as Father's quotation, into my notebook.

"Now this is strange," said Cody. "Either both quotes are about one person—a woman who went to the filing room—or they are about two separate people."

To us, Father's notes were so vague, but he must have known what they meant perfectly.

We were just about to continue when Cody jumped up with a start.

"Oh, girls, I've got to get home!" he exclaimed. "It's going to be time for dinner soon."

"Right," Fay replied, taking off the mittens Kodiak had lent her and returning them. "Besides, maybe if we take a break to refresh our minds, it'll help us think clearly for when we examine the next

51

part of the book."

"Sharp as a tack, Fay!" Cody stated with a snicker. "And thanks for giving me back my gloves."

Felicia laughed.

Putting the journal and things back in my bag, I thanked my friends for helping me with the work.

"Sure thing, Lia!"

In appreciation, I smiled at them. "We'll find it out; I'm sure of it."

Father, who had been gone for nearly five years now, was still helping us, in a way. If we could decipher his clues one at a time, and maybe get some extra information, that could be all we needed to discover the truth.

Still, it wasn't going to be easy. Each clue brought more questions, and we didn't know if our answers were accurate. That said, these clues demanded our attention. And if it *was* a murder, justice was at stake!

* * *

A few days later, I found myself walking down the sidewalk with my friends.

"I'm sure this will be a good idea," I told Cody and Fay.

We had decided it would be best to converse with our friend Uriah Harper. He was a man in his late twenties who was actually a private detective. In addition to that, he worked as a hired hand for the Nobleman ranch on occasion. Since solving mysteries was literally his job, what better person

was there to talk to?

Upon arriving at Mr. Harper's house, Cody rang the doorbell. Opening the door, Uriah looked a bit surprised to see us.

"Oh, Kodiak, Lydia, Felicia—what's up?"

"I'm sorry to just drop by," I apologized. "We need a quick bit of help on something. If we could have a moment of your time, that would be fantastic."

He quickly glanced at his watch and then smiled a bit. "Okay, I think I could spare a few minutes."

Inviting us in, Uriah led us to a table with some sprawled-out papers and things.

"Ignore the mess, please," he said. "I've been pretty busy working on a case, and things are getting a bit crazy."

"Oh," Fay breathed, "it's no trouble, but please pardon *us* for coming by when you're already so busy."

"Yeah," Cody agreed, having a dusting of pink on his cheeks from embarrassment for dropping in.

Uriah held up his hands and said with a slight laugh, "It's okay. Really, I need a quick break from this case anyway. It's driving me insane! So, what's the trouble?"

"Well…" I began slowly, "I'm confused about a mystery that occurred in Scottsbluff six years ago. I know you only moved to Wilsonville a couple of years ago, and that you were living in Kansas before that, but… Are you familiar with the death in the

53

Scottsbluff Aquatic Museum in 1999 on October twenty-first?"

A brief moment of reflection crossed Uriah's face, and then he said, "Yes, a little. I looked into it at one point but didn't see much information."

I nodded. "Mr. Harper, well, the thing is... I didn't know this at the time, but my father was trying to solve it."

Uriah's eyebrows shot up. "What?"

Reaching into my bag, I pulled out Father's journal. "Here, I found this book of my dad's, but I can't make sense of everything. He was writing stuff down, but eventually, it just... stops."

Mr. Harper inspected the journal.

Why didn't Father write anything else? I thought. *Did he abandon the case, or...?*

I bit my lip. Surely he didn't... pass away before he could finish it.

My eyes began to water, but I blinked furiously. This case was going to be solved. For justice's sake, and for Father's.

After looking through the pages, Uriah slowly handed the journal back to me. He hesitated a moment to speak.

"Lydia," he began, "no doubt your father was indeed looking into the case. I'm very interested in deciphering his writing once I solve the mystery I'm currently working on."

"But," said Cody, "is there anything you can tell us that maybe we could look into right now?"

In careful thought, Uriah was silent. The case was six years old, so he likely didn't think we'd get into danger if we tried to gather some clues.

"I believe you should just ask yourselves, 'Why?'" he said. "*Why* would Seth Arlington search into the case if he didn't have reason to think there was more to the story? If, for example, this is a murder case, *why* would this twenty-some-year-old woman have been killed? Murderers always have a motive."

Felicia nodded. "That's true. But it's so hard to find evidence, other than what's in the journal, because the case happened in Scottsbluff, which is nearly five hours away! And we don't really know whom to ask for details on anything, let alone the fact it's an old mystery."

"I know. But the thing with solving cases is that you always need to think of new ways to learn."

Certainly, he had a good point.

Cody tilted his head. "Hmm… Uriah, how do *you* do that?"

"Well, in a lot of different ways. Sometimes I take a step back and try to look at things more simply; other times I try to clear my head by going for a walk." He said this last part with a laugh.

Kodiak looked from Felicia to me. "Maybe we should take a walk too."

I smiled at my strawberry-blond friend. "It would probably be refreshing."

After conversing with Uriah for a bit more, we

then left, not wanting to take up too much of his time.

We had decided to follow through on Mr. Harper's advice. Beneath our feet, the snow crunched. As the three of us walked past the trees, I took in deep breaths of the chilly winter air.

The woods were serene.

No one spoke. We let nature make the tenseness of our search slip away. Or at least, Cody and Fay did.

While the woods were indeed peaceful, I couldn't forget about the book within my bag. As I walked, thoughts flooded my head.

Something was going on. But what?

I looked up toward the trees.

Gritting my teeth, I thought, *You don't even know if someone from the aquarium caused the death. Anyone could have, right? In fact, it might not have really been a murder!*

But no. I shook my head. It seemed to me that if Father was going to work to solve this case, he probably didn't think it was an accident or that whoever did the deed was a stranger.

Who was the culprit, then?

We had the list of workers for that day, of course, but other aquarium employees could've done it, too.

I was beginning to doubt myself. How could I really solve a case from six years ago that took place in a different city with suspects I hardly knew? It

seemed impossible.

Slowly, my eyes fell to my locket, inside which were two photos of my parents. Then, I recalled Uriah's words. He said he takes a step back sometimes. Maybe I needed to as well.

I had, without hardly being aware, walked off faster than my friends, who were now left behind. Upon turning around, I saw they were talking quietly.

Gradually, my head began to feel clearer.

Father wouldn't want me to give up, would he? Or Mother?

Gazing, I stared far off into the towering trees.

Then I recalled another phrase Dad had written in his book, which said, "What happened in the meeting room?"

It was no wonder I struggled with this mystery; I had been missing the forest for the trees. As if to grasp the big picture, I didn't try to wrap my head around the sentence itself too much. Instead, I tied it into the first two.

Father had written earlier that "she" could have gone to file. I decided to assume that hypothetically, "she" meant Liesel. Next, I added the part that he said about being north, then southeast. Naturally, Liesel would have been likely to come into the aquarium from the south, though, right? Because that was where the front entrance was. Which… led me to think… that someone *else* must have been north, maybe coming through the backdoor.

If "she" meant Liesel, then perhaps the twenty-three-year-old went to the filing room while someone else had come from north to southeast, entering the meeting room.

I gasped.

Of course!

Why would someone up to no good come through the front when they could come through the back? It would be easier to remain concealed if you entered from the north.

The filing room and the meeting room were right next to each other. Whoever was in the meeting room would have seen Liesel.

It appeared I had, perhaps, deciphered part of my dad's thoughts. But everything led to another question, which I didn't have an answer to.

Why was someone in there?

HE SAID EVERYONE HAS AN ENEMY

Chapter 5

It was the next day, and my grandma and I were conversing cheerfully. Currently, Grandmother was relaxing in the living room, crocheting a gift for a friend of ours, Nicole Miller.

"Did you know, Lia," began my grandma, "that I was talking to Nicole this morning and she gave me some wonderful news?"

"I didn't. What did she say, Grandmother?"

The older woman smiled, a twinkling in her eyes. "She informed me that she's had the immense

pleasure of courting Uriah Harper!"

I gasped in delight. "Courting? Oh really, that's just wonderful!"

My heart felt light. Uriah was previously going to be married to a woman, but his engagement had ended up being… called off. He was a fantastic person, and I had been hoping the best for him. Miss Miller would be perfect for Mr. Harper, I was sure, if they would continue. How excited Fay would be! And Cody too, of course, though Felicia was more interested in this type of stuff than he was.

I looked at my grandma with wide eyes. "Is it public news?"

She smiled with a slight nod, and I beamed back. Then I fell silent for a little bit, reflecting.

I needed to do something I was a bit hesitant about.

Sometimes, it hurt Grandmother and me both to talk about my parents, so neither of us did. But I had realized some years after their passing that keeping quiet didn't make anything hurt less in the long run. Occasionally, I tried to be more open with Grandmother, but sometimes it still felt uncomfortable to bring up memories—even if they were happy—because I didn't want to risk making *her* depressed and lonesome.

Would our loved ones want us to remember only bittersweetly? Or would they rather us recall without feeling pain? Oughtn't we also to have joy in the memories? I believed we should. So, was there a

60

way for me to find middle ground, where I missed them but could still hold them close to my heart? I could desire to be with them one day and be comforted by that thought. This world wouldn't be eternal.

I wanted to do something. I was determined to keep my parents' memory alive. So, even if it hurt, I knew it would be good for both me *and* for my grandma.

"Grandmother," I said softly as I crocheted, moving the deep-purple yarn underneath the hook, "how did you feel when Mother first started dating Father?"

She was quiet for a moment, and I was worried I made her sad, but it couldn't be helped. However, Grandmother then gave a slight smile, having a bit of a faraway look in her eyes.

"How did I feel?" she asked. "Why, Lydia, I felt so happy I could have burst with pure joy."

I was relieved that she didn't appear upset, and I let out a light laugh. Grandmother continued, "Seth was one of the finest young men I'd ever met. He was kind, a hard worker, reliable, and a dozen other things. But most importantly, his love for God guided his every action, which in turn made him the wonderful man he was. Your father and mother put the Lord first, above all else."

I sighed contentedly. "And may *I* always strive to as well."

Grandmother nodded in agreement, saying, "May

we *all*."

Quiet for a bit, each of us thought of the ones we loved and missed. Then I said slowly, "Grandmother?"

"Yes?"

"If I wanted to look at some files or things that were Dad and Mom's, where might I look?"

She raised an eyebrow at me. After a brief moment of consideration, she answered, "I'd imagine they'd be in some of the boxes in the attic."

Upon hearing this, I rose to my feet, my crochet long forgotten.

"Oh, Lia," she said with a slight laugh, "I think I know where you're wanting to go, but it's really getting late, and you'd better go to bed soon."

My eyes pleaded a little bit, but she smiled some, asking, "Tomorrow?"

I knew my grandma had a fair point because if I started looking now, I could lose all track of time, and then it'd *really* be late. But how hard it would be to rest when I felt so curious!

"All right, Grandmother," I consented. "Then I suppose I'd best go get ready to sleep."

As I turned to go, she stopped me for a moment.

"Lydia?"

"Yes, Grandmother?"

"You're still thinking about that journal of your father's, aren't you?"

* * *

Early the next day, I made my way up to the

attic. Patches of sunlight streamed in from the four small windows in the room, and I reached for the light-bulb chain, tugging it down a bit. The bulb was defective, and it flickered.

Beginning my search, I walked past some old furniture and then found a few boxes. They had various labels written with a marker. Upon seeing one with black writing over the top that read, "Seth and Liliana's records," I dropped to my knees, running my hands over the top. Some tears blinded me a bit, but I blinked them back and sighed.

Carefully, I pried at an edge of tape across the top of the box and peeled it slowly back, accidentally breathing in some dust on top and coughing.

Gently folding away the flaps on the box, I sighed heavily.

Perhaps I could find some other clues about the aquarium in my family's old files, which could lead to further evidence. It was most certainly worth a look.

There were a lot of different documents, which had been prudently sorted into different folders. Finding a few cases which were about my father's occupation, I pulled them out. I opened a folder that contained information for 1999 through 2001. Although the packet I held was bulky, I decided it would be best to look through each page, at least briefly, so as to not miss anything important. Once I pulled out a sheet of dates for Father's paychecks, my eyes skimmed through the years and months.

Tilting my head, I realized something seemed strange.

How unusual, I thought. *The amount of money for each paycheck started sinking in December of 2000? And then took a deep plummet in March of 2001, a month before his passing...?*

"Why would *that* happen?" I muttered aloud to myself. It didn't make sense. Father was always industrious, and whatever he set his hand to prospered.

I set the paper down by my side on the wooden floor and then sifted through the other documents.

After having searched half of the records, I realized how quickly time had flown. I'd be late for school if I didn't leave soon. So, I grabbed all the papers and left the attic. Putting the documents in my room, I decided to look through the rest once I got home.

As I was picking up my leather backpack, which had blue and white stripes on the flap as well as some lace, I asked Grandmother, "May I invite Cody and Fay over for a little while after school?"

She didn't even look surprised, quite used to that question, as my friends and I were always wanting to hang out. "Well now, I don't suppose I mind, Lydia," she replied with a small smirk.

I giggled a bit and thanked her. The two of us left the house—but not before I gave Charity some attention, which she was very grateful for.

Swinging open the passenger door, I entered my

64

grandma's snazzy, red convertible. Before long, we were driving through the little neighborhood. Unfortunately, Grandmother and I couldn't have the convertible's roof down because it was too cold.

Staring out the window, I tried to imagine how wonderful summer rides to school would feel again, with the breeze following through my hair and the sun on my face. But instead, all I saw were leafless trees, ice, and cold.

But still, winter had its beauties too. On a positive note, the snow did sparkle wonderfully, and the icicles gleamed. A single bird was perched on a leafless branch and seemed to be cheerfully surveying its surroundings. Even still, I couldn't enjoy this as much as usual because soon, my mind swirled around to the papers left at home—and especially the odd numbers on my father's paycheck records.

* * *

"Lia!"

Immediately, I turned my head toward the shout, as it sounded quite intense.

"Fay?" I inquired, perplexed. "What's up?"

I had just arrived at school. Upon seeing me, the curly-haired teen had pushed her way through the hallway of students, calling out with a most earnest look on her face.

"After we finished our walk a couple of days ago, I did some searching," she began.

My eyes widened. "Wait, and did you…?"

"Yes," Fay responded, nodding. "I found information."

"Well, what?"

"Blaire Forbes lives in Omaha."

I looked at Felicia, feeling a bit confused. That city wasn't nearby, anyway. Why did it matter?

However, she wasn't finished. "Miss Forbes may live in Omaha, but her *sibling* doesn't! Her sister has lived in Wilsonville this whole time!"

My jaw dropped.

"Really? Then wh-where?" I stammered. "What street?"

"She lives, like, two blocks from you."

At this moment, Cody came up to us.

"Hi girls," he chirped. "Ryker hit all the red lights on the way here, so he had to stop a lot, but I've arrived at last! Lia—what's with the shocked expression? You look like you've just seen a ghost. Did you really have such little faith in my coming?"

I composed myself and then laughed a little. "No Cody, it's not that. Please, tell him, Fay."

She explained, and Cody's jaw dropped just as mine had a moment ago. For a second, he forgot all else and said, "Well let's go see her, come on!"

"Kodiak," Felicia reminded gently, "we've got to go to class first, you goose."

"Oh. Right," the teen replied with a sheepish laugh. The three of us then headed down the hall, talking in quiet voices about the surprise as we did so. It was so hard to concentrate when we sat in our

66

seats and the class began, though!

With Miss Forbes's sister living near me this whole time, perhaps I could truly get some answers, as Blaire had been the one to find Liesel in the aquarium.

I tried to pay attention to our teacher, Miss Lewis, but when she called on me, I blushed and had to ask her to repeat herself. Cody shot me a sympathetic look from across the room; after all, *he* has always been prone to daydream only to get called on with no idea as to what was asked.

I rubbed the bridge of my nose and then shook myself a bit, trying to focus. Staring at the board, I sighed.

It was going to be a long day.

* * *

A lot of times, Ryker sat with Cody, Fay, and me during study hall since that was one of the few times we all got to see each other during the school day. But occasionally, Rhys would sit with his best friend, Micah Silvers, and some of the other seniors, and he was with them this day. I could see them across the room, planning some interesting group project.

As my friends and I sat down at a table, Felicia thumped an enormous book on the desk. Cody groaned.

"Oh relax, Kodiak," Fay said with a sigh and a wave of her hand, which seemed to say she thought he was silly. "I, for one, wish we were doing *regular*

algebra and not pre-algebra."

"Well *I* sure don't," Cody retorted. "This pre-algebra stuff is so weird, with all these added 'x's' and 'y's' taking up *everything*. Why not just keep it simple?"

"They're there for a good reason, though," Felicia said in the subject's defense. She then went on to explain the importance of algebra, and the two conversed for a while.

Tiredly and only half listening to my friends, I said, "I just wish I knew what that stuff in the attic was all about."

They both stopped their math discussion and turned to me.

"What stuff in the attic?" the teens asked.

I explained to my friends what was found earlier that morning.

"And so," I concluded, "none of it makes sense to me about Father's paychecks and all. There was no reason why he *should* have had a drop in funds. But then again, maybe that's just something I should investigate later. We've already got one case on our hands."

Cody looked deep in thought. "That is strange, Lia," he agreed. "By how much did his income drop?"

"In March, it fell by nearly thirty percent of what it was originally."

I heard an exasperated sigh behind me.

"Could you guys keep it *down*," Trevin seethed

at us. He and his friends had taken a table not far from ours.

Trevin Aragon was prone to getting annoyed at us for anything and everything, it seemed. Sometimes, he would get aggravated for no reason at all. And considering that my friends and I hadn't been very noisy in our discussion, this was certainly one of the times where it didn't make sense.

Cody paled a bit, always uneasy around Trevin Aragon. Then, the strawberry-blond boy's eyes narrowed, and he bit his lip. As if to calm his nerves, he took a deep breath.

"Pardon us, Trevin," Kodiak replied with an air of dignity. "We really ought to be studying, I suppose, but we are having quite a serious discussion."

Trevin gave an enormous eyeroll. "I don't care, you dunce."

"He is not a dunce!" Felicia retorted. She then blushed a bit from her outburst when some other kids turned around. I noticed that Ryker and his friends looked up.

"Keep it *down,*" Trevin hissed, glaring at Fay a bit. His own cheeks flushed in embarrassment. Some of his friends laughed a bit, which caused him to glare at them as well.

For a moment, Kodiak and Trevin squinted at one another in distrust, and the staredown lasted for what seemed to be a whole minute.

Eventually, Trevin turned back to his friends.

Cody then sighed, looking back at Felicia and me. "Let's get to work."

But just as we were starting, Trevin turned around to us again and, with a slight eyeroll, said, "Since you guys were *so* loud when you should have been studying, the whole room probably could hear you. So, unfortunately, I was forced to listen to your stupid conversation. Anyway, if *I* were you, I would be quieter. Plus, the only obvious way to know why someone's paycheck drops is to see the people they know. Everyone has an enemy."

I furrowed my eyebrows. He was giving us advice?

"Are you… trying to help us?" I asked slowly, with skepticism.

He looked at me with narrowed eyes. "Maybe. I don't really care."

The boy then huffed and, turning back to his companions, ignored our existence.

I stared at my two best friends, who looked as confused as I felt, and then I reflected on what Trevin had said.

Everyone has an enemy.

Was he right?

A ΠEW LiGH†

Chapter 6

At last, the final bell rang, so my friends and I hurried out of the building.

"Can you guys come to my house?" I asked.

A moment passed as the two teens thought it over, and then they both nodded.

"I can," replied Fay, "after I tell my mother, anyway."

Mrs. Blackwood was on her way to pick Felicia up.

"I'll let Ryker know I won't be riding home with him now," Cody explained.

When Grandmother came to get us, we piled into

the back. The three of us were mostly silent on the drive, but as soon as we got home, we headed to my room to discuss our plan—after thanking Grandmother for driving us and having my friends over, of course.

"I think we should go to Blaire's sister's house right now," said Cody.

Felicia nodded. "Since we *are* all together right now, it could be a good opportunity."

Glancing at my seahorse alarm clock, I added, "And we still have a while until you guys have to go back to your homes for dinner."

So, we left. It only took us a moment to put on our coats again, as well as our scarves and hats and anything else we could need.

Slinging over my shoulder the brown bag with the turquoise flap, I shut the front door behind us as we left, telling Grandmother we would be back soon.

Wilsonville is a small community, so my grandma wasn't very concerned about us biking or walking or doing anything by ourselves. People in Wilsonville look out for each other.

My heart raced as I headed down the street. I couldn't believe I had been living so close to the sister of Blaire Forbes all along! It took only a moment to arrive at her doorstep, and Cody knocked a clear, cheery knock.

About a minute later, the entrance opened, and a woman who seemed to be in her mid-twenties opened the door. She had light-brown hair with

matching eyes, and she furrowed her brow at us.

We waved and called out a "Hello!"

"Are you Miss Forbes?" I asked.

She looked a little surprised. "Why, yes. And who are you?"

"I'm Lydia Arlington. Please excuse my friends and me for interrupting you, but I live just a few blocks away and need your help."

Kodiak and Felicia introduced themselves too, and after a brief hesitation, the woman let us come in.

"I'm sharing this house with some of my friends—so roommates, basically," Miss Forbes explained. "Cassidy is out of town, but Jemma is cooking in the kitchen."

As she said this, a woman with blonde hair poked her head out of the kitchen doorway. "Hi there! Who are these visitors, Janet?"

"A girl from a few blocks away and her friends," Miss Forbes—or Janet—explained.

She led us to the dining table, the four of us sitting down. I half smiled briefly at her. "Miss Forbes—"

"Please call me Janet; everyone does."

"Janet," I said, slowly, "You're the sister of Blaire Forbes, correct?"

She looked a little confused but nodded and then asked if I knew her sibling.

Shaking my head, I replied, "No, but I would imagine my father did. He was the manager of the

Scottsbluff Aquatic Museum until his passing five years ago."

My heart seemed to sigh heavily within my chest as I said the last part.

Oh, Father and Mother, I miss you so much.

Miss Forbes gave me a sympathetic look, seeming to realize my melancholy.

"I'm very sorry," she softly said. Then after a moment's pause, she added, "My sister worked at the aquarium there, but what brings this up?"

I was careful with my next choice of words. "Janet... I... Well, did you know of a woman by the name of Liesel Allen?"

A brief flash of pain washed over her face. Giving one firm nod, she said, "Yes—yes I do. Or I did, before she died."

Cody almost jumped out of his seat, but he composed himself in time. "Do you know anything about it? How did it happen?"

Miss Forbes bit her lip in thought. "I'm not sure. I think she..."

The woman trailed off, then I saw her eyes brim with tears, and then they flashed.

"My poor sister found her! She's never been the same since," she said, shaking her head vigorously. "It wasn't fair!"

"Janet," Kodiak said in earnest, "how did it happen? Do you know?"

She gazed toward the ceiling in an attempt to keep her tears from falling.

74

"Blaire and Liesel were best friends. Those other employees—Trace and Ava and Zeb and Edith—they never bothered to be friends with them. They never *tried!*" she declared.

Fay's eyebrows shot up, and she opened her mouth to speak, but Miss Forbes continued.

"The day it happened—the day of the death—my sister and Liesel were driving together to work. It was Blaire's time to unlock the doors at the aquarium and get all the lights on. The workers were always instructed to bring another employee with them. One would go in while the other stayed outside and waited. That way, if the one who entered didn't come back in time, they would know something might be wrong."

I let out a shaky breath, feeling as if I could visualize the scene perfectly. Letting out a shutter, I waited for Miss Forbes to continue.

"Blaire was supposed to unlock the doors and put some papers up, but Liesel offered to because I had called my sister on the phone. The reason I called was that our father was old—he had married late in life, and age had made our parents feeble. Papa had a lot of health problems from his old age, and he was feeling awful that morning. I was so scared he was going to… leave us… and I didn't know what to do. When Mama and I had helped him recover, I felt compelled to call my sister and let her know what happened."

As if stifling a gasp, Fay put a hand to her

mouth, seeming to understand where the story was going.

"Well," Miss Forbes continued, "if I hadn't called, maybe Blaire would have gone in instead—probably—and then Liesel would have been spared, though I wonder if it would have been at my sister's expense."

Wait, I wondered. *If it would have been at Blaire's expense, then Janet must not think Liesel died because of her heart problems.*

"So," she said, "Liesel went into the building while Blaire searched the area from the outside in the vehicle instead. But toward the end of our conversation, she seemed nervous and said she didn't know why Liesel hadn't come out yet, so she hung up and then went to look inside. She found Liesel and... and..."

Her voice sounded pained, and I saw her eyes flash with anger again. "*They* did it! I *know* they must have. I hate them *all!*"

"Janet!" Jemma scolded, coming in from the kitchen and drying a bowl with a towel. "Don't say that, *please.* It's wrong to hate."

"I don't care if it's wrong—I hate them anyway! Liesel was always so nice to me. She was *kind.* When I was little, she'd let me play with her and Blaire. And when I was only seven, she even gave me her old porcelain doll, an old favorite of hers, just to make me happy."

At this moment, overcome with grief, Miss

Forbes held her face in her hands and burst into tears.

Even so, none of this gives Janet a right to hate.

"But," said Cody softly, "how do you know that she was murdered?"

"Edith didn't bother to show up at her *funeral* even though she had the day off," she choked out between sobs. "Not one of them so much as gave us a condolence!"

I furrowed my brow. That was strange, but it didn't mean that any of them had *killed* Liesel.

Jemma tried to console her roommate. Her expression suggested that she'd tried to speak with reason to the woman in the past but had long since given up.

"I hate them *all*," Janet choked out again. "It's not fair!"

Hysterically, she gasped out some more despairing words, saying, "I don't know what they did, but I know they did *something!*"

My friends and I exchanged glances, each feeling a little awkward as the woman carried on in this manner. I desired to leave.

"Miss Forbes—Janet," Felicia gently said, "I am truly sorry about your dear friend, but was there anything—any clues—that showed Liesel's death to be on purpose?"

"I don't *need* proof," she wailed. I was now getting concerned about our stay here. This woman seemed delirious, and glancing at my friends, I could

tell they were uneasy too.

"Janet," said Cody, slightly tilting his head to the side in reflection, "I believe—"

"No!" snapped the woman, and she put her head in her hands again. "No one needs any more evidence. I trust my sister's word."

"What?" Kodiak asked. "What did she say?"

"I think if a girl says she had this odd feeling, like she was being watched, as soon as she stepped into that building, that's all the verification you need to know it was one of those stuck-up employees!"

Cody was silent for a moment and then said as carefully as he could to prevent another flare-up from Miss Forbes, "I'm very sorry for your sister. But I'm afraid she didn't notice anyone other than her friend in the building?"

"She didn't need to," Janet replied simply with an air of indignance. Then, calming herself a little, she sighed. "Well… As far as I've ever known, my sister didn't see anything. Forgive me for my earlier outburst."

We nodded.

"I understand," responded Cody. "But she didn't notice anything? Not even a thing out of place?"

Miss Forbes fell silent for a moment, remembering. "Well… I think Liesel had only gone to file some stuff. But the light to the meeting room was on, and I think Blaire said the manager's office door was ajar."

Father's office?

Underneath the table, my hands carefully opened my bag. I reached for my notebook, where I had been recording clues. I quickly wrote a few notes, shut the book, and then closed the bag.

"So," Felicia began, interested in the case, "you think that Liesel did indeed go inside the filing room, correct? Was it open? Or why do you believe she went in?"

"When she entered the aquarium, she was intending to put up papers for Blaire, which I mentioned earlier."

"And it appears she did make it to the filing room unharmed?"

"Yes, the aquarium workers found her papers sorted in the proper cabinet."

I nodded. "Right."

After a bit more conversing, we left, not wanting to take up any more of Janet's time in addition to still feeling a bit uncomfortable around her. Walking down the sidewalk, I looked to Cody, then Fay, and asked them what they thought of our visit.

"I think Janet's filled with a lot of hate," Cody replied, looking a little relieved to be getting away from the house. "I feel bad for her, but still, she was so certain that one of the..."

His voice trailed off.

Giving a single nod, Felicia said, "Yes, she admitted that she didn't exactly have evidence but still accused the others of killing Miss Allen."

As we turned a corner, I pulled out my notebook,

skimming over the things I had written and adding a couple more points.

I then reached for Father's own journal in my bag and rubbed the bridge of my nose as I looked over his notes.

"Even though Miss Forbes shouldn't accuse them without evidence, something certainly does seem off about the case. I've been thinking for a while now that someone must have been in the meeting room, seeing as the light was on," I explained. "But that's not all, because it takes two people to have a meeting."

Cody nodded. "Right, so there were likely at least two people talking in there. They could have seen Liesel walk into the filing area since, on your dad's map, it showed you'd have to walk past the meeting room to get there."

Felicia looked at us with wide eyes. "But that leads to another mystery: What were they meeting about?"

That's a good question, Fay, but not the only one, I thought. *Why was the door to my father's office ajar?*

* * *

"Hold it out a little longer, Felicia. It's a half note, remember?" Ryker asked.

"Right," the curly-haired teen replied with a laugh. "I keep on singing it like it's only a quarter note, for some reason."

Ryker and Fay were practicing for their choir

while Cody and I were playing on his game system in the Nobleman living room. A few days had passed since we'd spoken with Janet Forbes.

Part of me wished to focus on nothing else but Liesel's case. However, Cody wanted to play the new game he'd gotten for Christmas while we waited on Rhys and Felicia, so I decided to temporarily let the mystery rest. It was nice to do some gaming with my friend. Besides, a break from the case would probably do all of us some good because, to be honest, my head felt like it was going to explode from so much thinking and wondering.

Cody shrieked and stared at me with a humorous face looking betrayed. Laughing lightheartedly, I said, "Come now, Cody, you usually win. So what if I managed to beat you just this once?"

Recovering from his horror, Kodiak then grinned cheerily. "Good job, Lia, you won fair and square. But let's have a rematch!"

The two of us proceeded, and I managed to give Cody an impressive run for his money. Unfortunately, the boy made a comeback in the end, causing me to lose.

After shouting dramatically, though only teasing, I said, "You got me."

"Take that!" he replied with a laugh, punching at the air.

"Let's play the game with the goblins."

Cody agreed and inserted a disc into his game system. The system was a little defective, sometimes

not reading the disc, so that he had to go through a bit of trouble, taking it out and putting it in again until the game finally started up.

We usually didn't play this one with Fay because she didn't like the monsters on it, even though they didn't really look scary. It was a lighthearted game, but anything involving goblins wasn't ladylike. Occasionally, Felicia would succumb, though, and I thought that, deep down, even she sometimes enjoyed the competition.

Kodiak and I chose our characters and then worked through the level, warding off evil bats that were in caves, jumping over traps, and cutting away at thick tangles of branches.

"Watch out, Lia!" Cody exclaimed. "Here comes the leader goblin!"

Ryker and Fay, distracted by our intense gaming, had ceased their practice altogether, holding their breath behind us. Yes, even *Felicia* was intrigued.

After a strenuous battle, Kodiak and I cheered loudly; the head goblin was defeated.

"Oh no!" shouted Rhys, and I turned to him inquisitively.

Seeing I deserved an explanation, the depressed teen explained, "You and Cross Eyes beat the high score that Micah and I set!"

Laughing gleefully, Cody teased his brother.

"Oh, come now, Pitchfork, clearly Lia and I are just better at this game than you guys."

"Kodiak Hugo Nobleman!" Ryker shouted in

reprimand. "Come back here!"

Rhys had intended to playfully tackle Cody, who jumped up and ran for the stairs.

"Don't use my middle name like that!" Kodiak shouted with a light blush on his cheeks. "You sound so scary."

Running up the stairs, Ryker smirked mischievously.

"Guys!" shouted Felicia, trying to bring reason back to them. "The scoreboard already shows who the *current* winner is. That doesn't mean it won't change later."

I backed her up. "You could still win!"

However, the two teens weren't really upset with one another; they just wanted an excuse to roughhouse. But at the sound of the commotion, Mrs. Nobleman entered the scene.

"Boys!" she exclaimed. "Please get away from the stairs. One of you could accidentally get hurt."

She had a point, and Ryker and Cody knew it. Submitting, they both carefully came down, though each smirked at the other a bit with looks that seemed to say, "I was going to win our roughhouse."

The corners of Mrs. Nobleman's mouth curved into a slight smile, as if she were also amused—even if she was a mature, grown woman.

"Now why don't the four of you do something a bit more unwinding," Mrs. Nobleman said.

"Like eating snickerdoodles?" Cody asked with a playful face.

She gave her son a look just as humorous as his, raising an eyebrow. "Now Cody, do you really think that's going to help you *calm down?*"

"No Mom, but it would be fun!"

As if in defeat, Mrs. Nobleman waved her hand up. "Okay, fine, help yourself. But just *one,* please."

The boy let out an enthusiastic shout and sprinted into the kitchen. Amused, Mrs. Nobleman shook her head, and then she invited us to join Cody in having a snickerdoodle ourselves. We accepted, thanking her enthusiastically.

The strawberry-blond teen was slowly eating his cookie, trying to make it last as long as possible.

"They're warm out of the oven!" he chirped, tilting his head toward the cookie sheet.

Opening the fridge, Ryker pulled out a jug of milk and poured the creamy drink into a tall glass.

"They're best with milk," Ryker said to himself happily, and then offered to get us glasses too if we wanted.

"I think I'll have to pass, Pitchfork," responded Cody. "My cookie's nearly half gone, and even still, there's something I love about snickerdoodles all warm and cozy out of the oven."

Fay laughed. "Warm and *cozy?* Kodiak, you *are* a rascal."

"Perhaps," he replied with an air of intelligence, "but I like to think I'm just a culinary expert. You know, actually, that milk does look delicious. Say, Ryker, pour me a glass after all. Who cares if it

makes the cookies cool down!"

"If you're such a culinary professional," inquired Felicia, "then why did you change your mind so fast?"

In a tone of voice that made Cody seem like he really *was* a famous chef, he went on to explain that one can still be an expert despite having changed preferences between warm cookies or dipped ones.

"Either way is fine," he wrapped up, "because it just varies on your craving at the moment. I usually save the leftover cookies—if there are any—for milk, though, because they've already cooled."

Thanking Ryker as he handed me a glass, I couldn't help but smile to myself. Spending time with my friends made the troubles seem to drift away. Already, my mind was feeling much more refreshed and ready to take on the riddle of 1999.

It was time to look at this mystery in a new light.

BULLiES

Chapter 7

In my mind, the words stuck out as sharply as
thorns.

Talking to myself, I muttered aloud, "He said,
'everyone has an enemy.' I wonder if..."

Certainly, Trevin Aragon had enemies, like that
boy who had been bullying him, Bastion. But was he
really trying to help me somewhat?

I never knew what to think of Trevin Aragon's
philosophies. Sometimes they appeared to make
sense, and other times... not so much. But
considering that I needed every clue I could get for
this strange case, I decided to at least consider his

words.

Trevin had said the phrase in response to overhearing my friends and me conversing about Father.

Biting my lip in thought, I headed up to the attic. As I tugged on the chain to turn on the light, I headed toward the box I opened not long ago when searching through papers.

Father's paychecks had taken a plummet shortly before his death. While I personally didn't remember that at the time it occurred—having been a rather young girl—there was something very unusual about such. After all, he was the *manager*, so why should the manager have been losing money?

Could my father have had an enemy at the aquarium?

Quickly, I sorted through all the papers in the box, trying to find some sort of clue. After working through them, I ripped open another box and then one more.

It took some time, but eventually, I had observed every paper. The only problem was that much to my dismay, I couldn't find anything unusual.

"Oh, what *was* it!" I exclaimed in bewilderment.

In an attempt to solve this, I searched over all the papers *again,* though it proved useless.

There was only so much I could do. If there wasn't any information here, then it didn't matter how many times I read and reread the papers; no noteworthy evidence would take place.

Rising, I began to pace the attic floor in thought.

Father shouldn't have been losing income. I'm pretty sure the aquarium was still making enough money, so what was causing him to go through this?

Perhaps my parents had been talking about this behind closed doors all those years ago, because I certainly didn't recall any of it.

My chest heaved out a sigh. Feeling grieved for Dad and Mom, I wondered what they were trying to shelter me from back then.

I could have handled whatever they had to say back then, right?

But… They kept it a secret. Of course, that was years ago, though! I was fourteen now and had been through enough to deal with any other distressing news that might be in store for me.

Having already acknowledged that there was nothing up here to serve my search, I sighed. Clearly, I would need to take my pursuit elsewhere. And there was only one place I could think of that might contain the information I needed.

It may be miles away, but if I'm going to get evidence, I've got to go to Scottsbluff Aquatic Museum.

* * *

Unfortunately, I couldn't go to the aquarium at that moment. After all, I had just been there not long ago, and it was miles away. However, I was in luck. Seeing what I would inevitably need to do, I asked Grandmother if she could take me there again soon,

and she agreed. It would be a month until we could leave, but I was in even *more* luck when she also decided to let Cody, Ryker, and Fay come with us!

In the meantime, I would need to work on other things pertaining to Liesel's case that wouldn't require my visit to the Scottsbluff Aquatic Museum.

"Hopefully there's extra information we can gather while waiting," I told Kodiak and Felicia as we walked through our school.

Fay nodded. "Maybe we can try to rule out some suspects or something."

"And Ryker could help us!" piped up Cody.

I grinned at my friends. "Then let's get him to hang out with us after school."

The two agreed, and we arrived at the lockers. With ease, I opened mine, pulling out a textbook and notebook, and Felicia did the same with her own locker. However, as we arrived at Cody's, he concentrated hard and fiddled with the lock to no avail.

"I'll never get used to opening this!" he moaned.

"Remember what Justice said," reminded Fay as she proceeded to meddle with the thing. "He said to treat it almost like you'd break it without *actually* doing so."

As mental calculations apparently began computing in Felicia's mind, she seemed to concentrate on the proper angle of her hand on the locker. And then, with one smooth motion, she opened it, beaming at Cody. "What did I tell you?"

"Oh, Fay!" the teen breathed. "You really *are* a rascal, but thanks!"

Quickly, Kodiak grabbed his things from inside and then shut the door. Resuming our walk, we turned a corner into our earth science class.

As we took our seats, I glanced over at Trevin Aragon, remembering his recent, possible clue.

What's up with that guy?

Seeming always arrogant, Trevin lifted his nose proudly in the air while studying. However, I thought he felt a little uneasy, deep down. In fact, despite his firmly pressed lips and cold eyes, that stared at the chalkboard as if silently scolding every unlearned student in the room, he looked rather pale.

Maybe he wasn't quite the teen he thought he was. *Appearing* one way and actually *being* that type of person are two different things, and I couldn't help but wonder if Trevin wasn't quite the tough person he acted like. Perhaps, he was even filled with many concerns and fears.

My eyes strayed to my friends, and after locking gazes with each of them, I tilted my head in a motion to Trevin. They caught on to my gesture, and then looked at him too. Returning their gazes toward me, their expressions seemed to say they thought the boy seemed unusual today as well.

Kodiak slowly mouthed out a "Let's follow him after class" and then cringed as the teacher called on him.

Oh no, Cody!

Feeling compassionate for my friend, I winced too. I shouldn't have distracted him and Fay!

Cody, frantically trying to answer the question the teacher asked, blushed deeply. Arrogantly, Trevin smirked a little at the teen's struggling, which annoyed me. I felt even more aggravated as some other kids in the backrow snickered.

However, the teacher appeared to notice the bullies and let Cody off the hook while glaring a bit at some of the unruly students. Kodiak let out an almost inaudible sigh of relief.

When the teacher asked who in the class would like to answer the question instead, Felicia offered quickly, with a sweet smile on her face.

With a tremendous eyeroll, Trevin let out a huff and resumed scowling at the chalkboard.

* * *

As the bell rang, my friends and I jumped up out of our chairs, thanked the teacher for the lesson, and gathered our belongings. Swiftly, we each turned on our heel and walked in single file out of the classroom.

Going into the hallway, we then walked beside one another in a horizontal line, with me in the middle.

"I don't know, guys," I said in a quiet voice. "Maybe we should just go on."

I didn't want to risk Trevin getting annoyed at us *again*.

"We could," Cody said simply, "but I don't want

to. Something's up with him."

Fay shrugged. "Something's *always* been up with him, Kodiak."

"That's true," the teen agreed with a nod of his head. "But still…"

He trailed off.

"Okay, fine," Felicia consented a little helplessly. "I'm with you on this."

She then was silent, lost in thought as we hurried through the halls. Abruptly, Cody ceased walking.

"What's up, Felicia?" Kodiak asked, eyebrows up. "You're very solemn."

"I was just reflecting on… when Trevin and I had that school project a long time ago, right after we all started going to school here in Beaver City. Mother made me invite him over to dinner so we could work on the project, and…"

Cody pressed his lips together, remembering. Back then, when Trevin and Fay had the project, Kodiak had been rather upset to find out that Felicia seemed to be hanging out with his own bully, even if it wasn't *quite* like that. Later, he eased up a bit after learning that she wasn't intending to "betray" us or anything and that she was rather distraught over it herself. Now, Cody calmly waited for her to continue with her thoughts.

"Well, sometimes when I was talking to him back then," Fay said softly, "he just seemed like a normal teen and not a, well, jerk. I don't know why he's so disagreeable."

Cody nodded. "Maybe there was a time when he used to actually be nice—well, like years and years ago."

Next, I spoke as we resumed walking. "I still wonder what Trevin meant, giving us that random advice about people having enemies."

Cody shrugged. "Who knows? But it's worth considering, I suppose."

We saw Trevin Aragon and his buddies standing together in a circle, conversing. They seemed upset.

As my friends and I went to my locker, which wasn't far from where the boys were standing, I quickly and silently did the combination. I overheard a bit of the bullies' discussion.

"Wait, that Bastion kid got into a fight with your big brother?" angrily exclaimed one of the boys to Trevin. He sounded astonished.

"Yeah. So, I'm skipping out a few days of school."

"It's that bad, Trev?"

"Mom wants Joshua to rest for a while after getting so... Well, someone's got to fill in for my brother at the general store—and that someone's *me* because I'm the oldest after him."

"Well, what'd Bastion beat him up for, man?" asked another of his friends.

"I don't know for sure; I think he's mad about my dad or something. Dad's got the job his father always wanted."

"But I thought he was making fun of you for

being poor?"

"Don't call us *poor,*" I heard Trevin snap. "We're doing fine, you hear? And yeah, well, to be honest, Bastion's dad doesn't make that much money either; he just wants everyone to *think* his father does. Really, we all know his mom works too."

The group talked together for a while longer, some almost shouting in rage for the mistreatment of their friend's family. I closed my locker and then exchanged glances with Cody and Felicia. Clearly, they had heard the conversation as well.

"Let's get out of here," I whispered.

* * *

"So, it appears to me that Trevin's got his own share of problems also," said Fay.

The three of us were working on homework in her room.

Kodiak looked up from an algebra equation and took a sip of his strawberry milk. "Who would have thought that *my* bully was also getting bullied?"

As he finished the sentence, I reflected on when I had seen Ryker help Trevin out. Deciding it best to let my friends know, I filled them in.

"Still," I said, "I can't believe that Bastion guy and Trevin's brother were fighting. It's ridiculous! Bastion seems like nothing but trouble."

The two agreed, and then Felicia asked me for my notebook. Reaching into my bag, I pulled it out, handing the thing over.

94

"I want to look over your page of workers from 1999," Fay explained, who had just finished her homework a couple of minutes earlier. "Perhaps we can narrow the list."

At this moment, I heard someone coming up the stairs, and before long, Ryker Nobleman entered the room. We'd been planning to spend time with him, after all, and so he also had come to Felicia's house. However, he had been hanging out with Miles Carpenter while we did our homework.

"Hi, Pitchfork!" Cody chirped.

"Hey, guys!" Ryker greeted us. "Miles just left to go back to his house. So, what's up?"

"Oh, really? I thought he was staying for dinner," Felicia explained, a little surprised.

"I think he was going to but ended up leaving early to study stuff with a friend."

Ryker and Fay conversed a bit more on the topic, and then Felicia set back to work, skimming over the various names I'd written down before. After a period of silence, she said, "It doesn't seem like we can exactly shorten the list, but I suppose we can at least go over it. Is it okay if I write in here, Lia?"

I nodded. "Have at it."

She made three categories.

"This column on the left is for Liesel Allen's supposed friends," Felicia described. "And this one in the middle is for neutral relationships, and *this* one over here is for people we know she *didn't* get along with."

Cody, his homework now forgotten, sat next to Fay, looking over her shoulder at the list.

Felicia went on to carefully write each name in its section. Her finished work showed Blaire Forbes in the "Friends" column. Next, since Janet Forbes had said Ava Taylor, Trace Turner, Zeb Bayer, and Edith Webb (now Edith McKenzie) weren't very friendly with Liesel, wrote them down in the "Opposing" column. Finally, Fay put my father and Hezekiah Colville's names in the "Neutral" section.

"Now, all of this should be accurate—assuming those we talked with were telling the *truth*," explained Felicia.

"Okay," I said. "But I still have something on my mind."

My friends looked at me with an expression that asked me to continue.

I did so, saying, "How do we know Liesel was killed for *personal* reasons?"

Cody looked a little confused. "What do you mean?"

I let out a soft sigh. "Just suppose she was in the wrong place at the wrong time or something?"

Fay gave one slow nod, thinking. "That's true. But I imagine this list could still be useful. For example, I feel that it wouldn't be likely for a friend of hers, like Blaire Forbes, to be guilty of her death—assuming they really were friends."

"Right," I agreed. "So, if it's anyone on this list, it's likely either Ava Taylor, Trace Turner, Zeb

Bayer, or Edith Webb."

Ryker, glancing at the names on the paper, tilted his head. "It could be Mr. Colville, though, right?"

"I suppose it's possible," I consented, "but I don't know. He's a family friend, and I can't imagine him harming anyone."

Cody gave me a sympathetic look and said gently, "Yes, but that's what we've thought before. Appearances can be deceiving, even among friends."

The memories of our past adventures—if you could call them adventures, as they were more like nightmares—made me feel uneasy, and I shook a bit. "I know, Cody. I'll at least consider it, I guess."

A long silence ensued, each of us likely reflecting on our pasts. Eventually, I—my throat clearing and heart thumping a little—began to say something that felt almost unreal. "Guys, there's something I've been wondering."

My three friends looked at me attentively. I took a moment to fill Ryker in on any information that we hadn't told him yet, and then said, "I'm wondering if my father's drop in income and Liesel's death are connected."

They all stared at me with wide eyes. Then, after some thought, Cody spoke.

"Then, maybe we need to focus on finding out about your father's job. And that may, in turn, tell us about Liesel."

Nodding, I agreed. "Let's look for ways to learn more. I've already searched through all the papers in

my attic, but I didn't find anything of importance other than what we've already been discussing."

"Maybe your grandmother would know something," Felicia said. "Or perhaps... even Ryker and Cody's parents, and mine."

She had a great idea. We could each talk to our families. And as I considered it more, perhaps there was even someone else I knew that I could speak with.

"I think there's a man in particular that we should see. Do you remember... when we were searching to find out what happened to my parents, how we met someone who had also been trying to discover the truth alongside Uriah?"

"Oh, *yes!*" Felicia breathed, recalling. "Mr. Adam Bennet!"

Ryker's face brightened. "Of course, Lia—your father's best friend."

Mr. Bennet is a kind man who lives in Cambridge. As had just been mentioned earlier, he also had been Dad's best friend. After my family died, I hadn't seen him for about three years, but Grandmother and I had spent time with him more frequently since then. In his presence, I felt a bit of comfort, knowing that he had once been so close with my father.

If any candidates other than Grandmother would know what was up, then Adam Bennet, Mr. and Mrs. Nobleman, and Mr. and Mrs. Blackwood would qualify.

"So, do me a favor, please," I asked my friends. "Talk to your parents about this soon, and then let's meet up and see what we know."

The three teens nodded in agreement, a look of determination in their eyes.

TWO CASES ROLLED INTO ONE

Chapter 8

"Grandmother?" I asked.

She was crocheting an afghan square for a blanket. Looking up at me and pausing her work, my grandma asked, "Yes, Lydia?"

"I need help with something."

With a small smile, Grandmother motioned for me to sit down on the couch next to her. After I did so, the two of us stared at one another, and then I blurted out, "Grandmother, what happened to Father and Mother?"

This took her aback.

Flushing a bit, I realized that wasn't quite what I meant to ask. "Excuse me. Particularly, what I intended to say is… Well, I found some papers, Grandmother—papers that show there was something off with Father's paychecks before he and Mom died."

My grandma gave an incredibly surprised expression at this. Setting aside her afghan square, she then looked me straight in the eyes.

"Lia," she said, gently, "Seth did lose money."

I felt perplexed. "Why'd it happen?"

Grandmother shook her head in uncertainty. "As far as I'd known, none of us ever knew why."

"Couldn't he have asked his boss for an explanation?"

After all, Father was the manager, but someone was still over him.

Grandmother simply shrugged and said, "He did, but he never got an answer."

What? That's so strange.

"How could they not answer him?" I questioned, feeling extremely confused. "That's not very fair. He should have a right to know about his own income!"

"Indeed, Lydia, he certainly should have."

"Do you have any idea of what it could have been? Any speculation?"

My grandma thought for a moment, then replied, "I'm not sure. Either it was a miscommunication, or perhaps… someone was against him."

I knew that something was definitely up. There must have been stuff going on behind the scenes. Just what?

Slowly, I said, "Don't you wish you knew?"

"Of course I do. But at the same time, my daughter and son-in-law have already been gone for nearly five years now…"

Grandmother heaved a heavy sigh and looked away as if to hide her tears. I felt a little concerned that I shouldn't have brought anything up. Upsetting her was something I hated to do.

"I'm sorry, Grandmother, I—"

"Oh, Lydia," she said, wiping her tears away on her sleeve. "Don't apologize. There's nothing wrong with you asking about your parents. You *deserve* to be able to talk about them. We both do."

I opened my mouth to speak, then closed it. All I could do was smile in thanks to her.

Then she said, "Let's keep our memory of them alive."

I tried to swallow the lump in my throat. Letting out a gasp, I hugged her and exclaimed, "Oh, Grandmother, thank you! It hurts to talk about them sometimes for me, too. But I don't want to stop myself from remembering them. It's a horrible feeling, isn't it? Never speaking about them—it makes things feel almost as if they never lived."

"I know what you mean, child." Then she let out a soft laugh. "I suppose I can't call you that for long; you're a teenager, after all."

Releasing the hug, I replied gently, "Let's talk about them, Grandmother—about Mother and Father."

* * *

Since Adam Bennet lived in Wilsonville, I biked to his house. It was Saturday, so Mr. Bennet would most likely be available, but one could never be sure.

Felicia and I were having a sleepover that night, and so she was actually with me. Parking, we then walked up to his front door, hoping he'd be home. As I knocked on the door, I was much relieved when Adam appeared at the entrance. He was quite surprised at Fay and me showing up but seemed happy to see us, inviting us in.

"I didn't expect to see you today, girls! What brings you by?"

"Oh, Adam, I hope you don't mind us dropping by uninvited, but I was hoping you could help me with something about Dad that I'm really perplexed about."

He was even more surprised by this but was willing to be of assistance. Felicia and I took a seat opposite Adam on one of his couches. For a moment, I was silent as I thought through how I wanted to phrase things.

Finally, I said, "Adam, I was searching through some old records of my parents and found that Father's income... Well, shortly before his passing away, his income from Scottsbluff Aquatic Museum just *dropped*."

Mr. Bennet had been listening to me with the utmost intensity, and I couldn't read his expression, for it was like a stone. He waited for me to continue.

"I can't see any reason why his income *should* have dropped, seeing as Father was such a hard worker," I explained. "But also, I imagine you might recall how a woman named Liesel—Liesel Allen—was found, not more than a year and a half earlier… *gone.*"

A shiver ran up my spine at my last word.

"And so," I resumed, "I began to think that maybe the two occurrences were actually connected, even though they each took place at different aquariums, because there is one factor that ties them both together: Father."

Now, Fay spoke.

"Mr. Bennet," she earnestly said, "we know you were Mr. Arlington's best friend. So, if he entrusted you with knowledge, and you can let us know *anything,* we'd be so very grateful. We're confident he was trying to solve the case about Liesel, and we're trying to solve hers and *his.*"

Our story with its wish now finished, we waited in silence for him to reply.

"Girls…" he said softly, and I thought he seemed saddened, recalling his dear friend. "Seth confided in his family and closest friends, and I am honored to have been considered his best friend. He did confide in me about his income."

I can't describe how I felt at that moment. What

had happened in 2001? What was I finally going to learn?

"Did Father have... an enemy?" I asked Adam Bennet, the dreaded words making me hold my breath.

"I don't think he himself fully knew why his income was shrinking," Adam clarified. "But I'll explain to you what Seth told me, and hopefully it'll help."

A moment passed as Adam recollected his thoughts from five years prior.

"He was distressed," Mr. Bennet began, "almost like... Well, actually, let me back up. First off, Seth was trying to solve the case from 1999, as you both thought. He was the manager, you know, and I think the thought of one of his *own* employees dying really grieved him. I think he felt like maybe he could have prevented such a thing from happening, even though as far as I see things, that'd be impossible."

I nodded.

Resuming, Adam said, "Seth had informed me a little about his thoughts on things, but I don't think he ever reached a definite conclusion, as close as he may have come."

Pulling my notebook out of my bag, I then turned to a fresh page, ready to write down any information I could.

"Seth believed there was a troublemaker at the aquarium," Mr. Bennet said flatly. "However, I don't think he ever supposed *his* case of disappearing

income was connected to *Miss Allen's* death."

Felicia turned to me with wide eyes. "Which… means that if they *are* connected, it'd be no wonder Mr. Arlington's search hit a dead end. His own problems may have been the clues he needed to solve the original case."

As I heard these words, my heart skittered, upset. Fay had a point.

Adam gathered his thoughts again and continued, "Seth was unsure, but he felt someone perhaps was slandering him."

Quickly, I wrote that fresh information down and then said, "Do you know if he had any idea who that person may have been?"

Adam shook his head. "I don't. In my opinion, it seems someone was up to no good. I just wish I knew the motive."

I was, most likely, dealing with two cases rolled into one, which now meant that… I needed to discover why someone would have been against my father.

* * *

Felicia and I were in my room, sitting on the bed while making friendship bracelets. My dog, Charity, was lying at my feet. Knotting pink embroidery floss over purple thread, Felicia said, "Even though Father told me your dad confided in him about some of the income problems, they still seem quite unsolved."

In agreement, I replied, "That's what I've been thinking, Fay. Unless Cody's had any luck with *his*

parents, we're going to have to dig deeper."

"At least Adam was rather helpful."

"Certainly," I agreed, my hands tugging on the strings of my own embroidery floss, which were the same color as Felicia's. We were making matching bracelets to give to each other. The reason we picked pink and purple was that the former was Fay's favorite color while the latter was mine.

Weaving her hands through her strings, my friend pondered the enigma.

"Your father was a wonderful man," Felicia said. "I can't imagine why *anyone* would ever want to cause him harm."

"Yet it seems people found reasons," I responded sadly, thinking not only of the income struggles my parents had faced but even more so of their murder, which felt far worse.

It was at this moment that the phone rang. Rising to get it, I then stopped short upon hearing Grandmother answer, talking cheerily to the person on the other end of the line. As I was about to resume my bracelet-making, Grandmother came in, saying the call was for me.

Quickly, I left the room, grabbing our home phone and saying, "Hello?"

A familiar teen's voice greeted me back on the other end of the line—Kodiak Nobleman.

Smiling a bit, even though he couldn't see me, I asked, "What's up?"

The boy went on to tell me that he had talked to

his parents about my father, and that they had known about the income (as Fay's family did), but that the cause was unsolved. I somewhat expected this news and thanked him.

Instead of hanging up, Cody also explained that he was thinking, wondering if perhaps we should discuss this with our detective friend, Uriah Harper.

It seemed like it could be a good idea, assuming we'd be able to spare a few moments of the sleuth's time. Agreeing with Cody, I then talked about the matter a little longer before he needed to go help Rhys with some chores.

After returning to my room, I explained everything to Felicia.

"I think that'd be a lovely idea, to see Uriah," she approved, finishing up the friendship bracelet.

"Then it's settled."

Yet, I couldn't help but worry that maybe even Uriah, who literally worked as a detective for a living, wouldn't be able to help us. A plan was better than nothing, however.

* * *

"Mr. Harper," I asked, "what would you suggest we do?"

My friends and I had asked Uriah if we could spare a few moments of his time, apologizing most lavishly for interrupting him from his work. We tried to get to the main point of our conversation as quickly as possible.

Having filled Mr. Harper in on the whole story,

we were now mute, waiting for his advice. As we did so, he surprised us by getting up and pacing the floor.

"It does sound like bad business," Uriah agreed. "I can see why'd you'd be desperate to search for the truth."

Cody tilted his head. "Do you think the cases are connected, then?"

"It's probable."

A pen with purple ink in hand, I was ready to record any information in my book.

Uriah then came back to the table, seating himself. "I think," he said, "that we should first make a list of possible motives."

It seemed like a useful idea.

"I'll start," said Uriah. "Jealousy could be a potential reason."

"Maybe the motive was to help someone," suggested Felicia.

Beginning a list, I wrote those two down on my sheet.

"Oh!" Cody piped up. "Perhaps a motive could be greed? Maybe the money was *stolen*."

Quickly, I added that, too.

"What about… *revenge?*" I asked and then shuttered a little. I hated even saying the word, but we needed to consider any motives.

Uriah nodded in agreement. "That could be one; write it down."

I did so. This list seemed useful, as we each

knew that someone might act on such motives.

"Maybe it's to hide a secret."

The four of us turned to the unexpected voice and let out a slight gasp. "Ryker?" we exclaimed. "What are you doing here?"

Ryker laughed merrily at our reaction but then grew sober.

"Sorry for just barging in—I think you forgot to lock the front door, Uriah. Anyway, these are for you."

The teen then proceeded to place a plate of frosted cookies in Uriah's hands.

"They're from your girlfriend," said Rhys bluntly with a smirk. "While I was out running errands, I bumped into Nicole, and she said she was going to give you these tomorrow at your... date?"

Cody snorted out a laugh.

"But," said Ryker, looking at Kodiak in amusement before turning back to Uriah, "since I was going to be driving past your area, she asked if I could deliver these cookies to you now so you could have them early."

Uriah blushed, but I could tell he was pleased.

"Thanks, Ryker. Won't you chat with us for a bit?"

"I'd love to, but Mom needs me to get back with the groceries. Be seeing you guys! Oh, and good luck."

With that being said, the teen waved and then left.

Uriah set the cookies (which Cody probably wished were snickerdoodles) on the table and then resumed.

"So, this list is just to help you think of *why* someone may commit a crime; it doesn't mean they necessarily *possessed* any of these intentions," he explained. "But still, think about each one carefully, and see what adds up."

"Thank you, Mr. Harper," we said.

"Of course, and good luck. Here, let me show you something."

Uriah rose and motioned for us to follow him. We did so, and he led us through a hallway, where he opened a door. Entering, I let out a slight gasp.

Inside the room, there was a table in the center, buried with papers. The right wall had a bookshelf pushed up against it, filled with study materials of all sizes. Turning to my left, I gazed at a corkboard covered with articles, papers, and sticky notes, pinned in place. A trash can in a corner of the room was filled to the brim with wadded-up papers, likely tossed with much frustration.

In complete amazement at the sight, my jaw dropped, and a look toward my friends' direction showed me they had a similar reaction.

"This," Uriah began, "is how I think."

"It's remarkable," I gasped. "How do you do this?"

He let out a slight laugh, a little embarrassed at our amazement. "By collecting as much evidence as

I can, and then piecing it in, bit by bit, until everything comes into focus."

Felicia, so fond of knowledge, walked toward the corkboard of ideas. "What type of case are you working on?"

"A robbery in Lisco," answered Uriah. "If my suspicion is correct, I should only need one more piece of evidence for everything to fall into place."

I came near him, a slight smirk on my face. "How far you've come on this case is extraordinary; Nicole Miller must be proud."

A slight dusting of pink spread across his cheeks, and I smiled at him. His own lips curled into a similar look.

Giggling in glee, Felicia turned to us upon hearing my statement. "Oh, Mr. Harper! I *am* so excited for you."

Even Cody looked a little enthused and said, "I've had Nicole's cookies before, and they have my full approval. As long as you still make time to play basketball with me, I'm all for you and Miss Miller."

I could tell the strawberry-blond teen was mostly jesting, as he likely would have been in approval regardless. Thankfully, any of Kodiak's fears were pushed away, though, when Uriah cheerfully agreed to still be available for his young friend. He even offered him a cookie! With all the time Mr. Harper spent at his side job on the Nobleman ranch, the two had become rather close.

For a while longer, the three of us talked with

Uriah, and then we headed out, not wanting to distract him too much from his current case.

* * *

The days rolled on, yet with no more luck.

It didn't matter what I did, whom I talked to, or how many times I read over my father's notes; I couldn't find anything—not another clue *at all*—and was left only to speculation.

In about a week, I'd be going to the aquarium. But even then, would I really be able to find any answers, or would my visit there be in vain?

Rarely in my life had I felt myself lose hope, but this was a time when I did.

After all, I thought, *if Father couldn't find it out, why should I expect myself to? He was older than me, and wiser.*

"Lia? You're awfully silent."

I turned to Felicia as she said this. The three of us were hanging out at her house while she was beating Kodiak in chess. Ryker wasn't with us due to the fact his best friend, Micah Silvers, had invited him over for some intense gaming. I was going to join in on the chess game with Fay after Cody lost, and I had just been watching them as their "audience." But, while spectating for some time, I had got caught up in my own thinking, losing focus on the match.

"It just feels… impossible," I said in response to Felicia, "trying to solve this whole case. It's like we're never going to solve it."

Cody, eyes wide, jumped up from his seat, nearly wrecking the chess pieces off the board by accident.

"We'll figure it out!" he shouted. "You've got to have hope, Lia."

I stared at him for a long while, still feeling uncertain. But then, thankful for his confidence, I let out a tiny smile.

Felicia backed Kodiak up. "We've been through this stuff before, and we got through it. We'll get through it this time as well—together, as always."

Just because we solved cases before didn't mean we'd solve this one, though. Truly, I wanted to believe my friends, but at the same time, I didn't want to be disappointed if things didn't work.

The ones who lost Liesel need our help... They need their mystery solved—and I need mine answered, too.

Continuing, Fay said, "I think each of us has doubted ourselves from time to time in the past. We've each had a mystery hit close to home, after all, and I think when it feels so personal, we can get even more anxious about solving it."

Cody agreed with her and then gave me an encouraging smile, saying, "*Uriah* doesn't give up, remember? He works hard, and we have faith in him."

Felicia nodded. "So now, have faith in the three of us—yourself included. Okay, Lydia?"

My friends had a point, even if we weren't official detectives like Mr. Harper. I decided to

believe in them. It would be better to try and fail than to never take the risk.

"When I first tried to solve this case," I began, "you guys were with me from the start. You've both *always* been here for me, and now *I'm* going to believe in you—in *us*."

My two friends beamed at me, and I beamed back.

Taking a deep breath, I added, "Cody? Fay? You guys are right. Too much is at stake to give up now! Let's do this for Liesel Allen's family and for her friends."

We felt a new determination wash over us, one stronger than ever before.

"And," I closed, "let's do this for Father and Mother."

A Final Chance

Chapter 9

I slung my bag, carefully packed with Father's journal and my own notebook, over my shoulder. Hours earlier, Grandmother, Ryker, Kodiak, Felicia, and I had left in my grandma's convertible for the aquarium. Having finally arrived at our destination now, we scattered out of the vehicle. As I had done a couple of months ago at the very beginning of my search, I stared at the building in front of me.

Here I am again, Father, Mother… If only you each could know what we might be uncovering…

It felt that the entire case relied on this day. If I couldn't find any information here, I didn't have the

slightest idea where to look next. At best, we would postpone the mystery to a future date; at worst, my friends and I would never solve this enigma.

Taking a deep breath to steady my nerves, I then exchanged encouraging glances with my three friends as we walked together through the parking lot.

When we arrived at the front of the building, Ryker held the door open for us, and we entered.

"Lydia Arlington! Hello!"

I turned toward the familiar voice and saw none other than our family friend, Hezekiah Colville. Cody's words of prudence, "Appearances can be deceiving, even among friends," resounded in my mind. However, I still smiled as warmly as I could at Mr. Colville and shook his hand. The others did the same.

As he did last time, our friend offered to escort me to any of the rooms I might wish to see. That was just what I was hoping he'd say, of course, and it was almost as if Mr. Colville had read my mind. We'd go after he finished some current work.

In the meantime, my grandmother, my friends, and I walked through the building, looking at the various sea creatures. As we reached the section of the building with the reef tunnels, my heart skipped a beat. Memories flooded my mind of being here so many times in the past with my family, and my eyes watered.

A magnificent whitetip reef shark swam in the

exhibit, and I held my breath.

"*Oh,*" Felicia inhaled, looking through the glass behind me, "aren't the eels so stunning?"

"They sure are, Fay!" Cody chirped, standing next to her. "The pufferfish are my favorite, though."

And my favorite are the whales—as were yours, Father.

It would have been pleasant to go to one of the other exhibits in the aquatic museum to see whales and other huge marine life, but for now, I took in the beauty of the reef creatures.

Mother had adored starfish. And she loved the sturgeons, which were also Ryker's favorite. Although nothing could top whales for me, sturgeons were certainly a close second place.

Gently, a soft sigh escaped my lips, and despite the bittersweet memories, I tried to enjoy myself. Concealing any pain from my friends, I began chatting with them about the different creatures. Usually, chatting with Ryker, Cody, and Fay helped me push aside my dreary feelings.

After a while of walking through the tunnels and taking in the wonders of the sea, we then entered the jellyfish room, my grandma's favorite exhibit.

These creatures in particular were amazing, and all five of us watched them in awe. Scottsbluff Aquatic Museum, as well as the other aquariums I frequent, always reminds me of just how amazing God is to make such a vast variety of stunning beings.

Once we were about to proceed to the exhibit for large marine life, where I could see the whales, Hezekiah Colville found us and said he was ready to escort us. Deciding it best to temporarily postpone seeing the large creatures, we agreed. Mr. Colville spoke cheerily as he led us through the staff offices and asked if we would like a formal tour of the various rooms.

After all, although my friends *had* been through these rooms before, it was a long time ago, and he figured they might like to see it again after such a long absence.

We accepted the tour, so Hezekiah took us through each room, introducing everyone to the various staff members. I mainly wanted to get to the filing room, where I felt I'd have the best luck at retrieving evidence, but I patiently enjoyed the socializing as much as possible.

Mr. Colville found us all very trustworthy. So once his tour was over, he was kind enough to let us look around wherever we wanted, without his escort, and told the employees to let us do so. As I could now look through the files without any interruptions, *this* was certainly something to be glad about.

Ignoring the large sign that showed the room was only for the staff (since I was allowed to go in), I entered the filing room. Cody and Felicia followed me while Ryker chatted with Grandmother. I could tell my grandma was speaking to him about the manager's office, which had once been her

son-in-law's.

Just like when I had come to the aquarium a couple of months ago, Zeb Bayer was in the filing room. There was also another employee in there, a guy who seemed to be about Mr. Bayer's age. The two were apparently friends, and they were talking happily about Trace Turner's engagement to Ava Taylor as they worked. I recalled Edith McKenzie saying Trace was Zeb's best friend.

"I still remember when Trace and Ava first met," said Mr. Bayer, skimming through a paper. "I knew they'd be perfect for each other."

Whispering to me, Cody said sarcastically, "What a romantic way to put it..."

Fay rolled her eyes at our friend, though playfully.

More casually than Zeb, the man asked absentmindedly, "Didn't they start going out around the time you got that new position? It seems Trace and Ava have been dating for a long time."

Always interested in weddings and such, Fay looked as if she wanted to hear the conversation more. But my friends and I knew just what we needed to do: look for records about my father. There was no time to waste!

Quickly, Felicia found a folder labeled "Seth Arlington" and began opening it. The three of us carefully took a stash of papers from inside to look through.

As we each finished looking through our pile, we

exchanged glances in dismay.

Have we really come so far, only to find nothing more than we've already known?

Nothing in these documents taught us anything new.

"Maybe," Cody whispered, "we aren't looking in the right place."

We found another folder with records about my dad, but searching through them proved fruitless as well.

"No," said Kodiak. "I mean, maybe we're looking for the wrong *thing*."

Suddenly, it clicked.

"Code," I said softly, "do you mean we maybe need to look for records about the *others?*"

He gave one firm nod.

Felicia went to a different part of the filing shelf and said, "Let's see things from 2001."

There was certainly a lot of looking to do here, sorting through countless records. Thankfully, while we were doing so, another worker came inside, calling Zeb and his friend out to help with something in the water quality lab. Kodiak, Felicia, and I had the whole room to ourselves!

"Guys!" Fay urgently shouted. "*Look.*"

We all huddled around the papers in Felicia's hands. Quickly, I too noticed what she had. I exchanged looks with my friends.

"This can't be a coincidence, can it?" I asked. "Four workers quit working in 2001—in February."

"Were they fired?" Cody wondered aloud.

Pointing to the end of one of the records, Felicia said, "It shows here they left of their own will."

It was all so strange.

"Why?" I asked. "Why would they quit?"

My friends shrugged in bewilderment. Since Felicia was busy searching for further records on this odd occurrence, I pulled out a stash of folders from April and May of 2001.

Looking through the papers, I then stared at a single record. It was the list of workers for that month and each of their positions.

Quickly, I rose from my place and went to look at documents from March of that year.

I then clearly saw what was out of place—what didn't make sense.

My father had passed away in 2001, in April. The records after his passing show that Hezekiah Colville took his place as manager. He still was, of course. However, the documents from *before* Father's passing showed Hezekiah Colville *wasn't* Father's *assistant* manager. So why did he take Dad's place after his death? Shouldn't Father's assistant manager have taken the position? And who was his assistant manager, anyway?

While my friends continued to look through the other files together, I slipped out of the room.

Walking through the hallway and toward the manager's office, I stopped short. Grandmother and Ryker were no longer nearby. Likely, they had gone

back toward the sea exhibits, perhaps to see the whales. It may have been that they'd expect Cody, Felicia, and me to meet them there, considering we hadn't reached that exhibit yet.

Silently, I pushed open the door to the manager's office, which had once been my father's. In the center was a table with various papers sprawled out on it. Also on the table was a framed family photo of Hezekiah and his wife along with their grown kids and their families. Remembering how Father once had a picture of Mother and me on his desk, I smiled bittersweetly.

Although I had permission to go into all the rooms, I didn't necessarily have the right to snoop through Mr. Colville's things. And besides... I wasn't suspicious of Hezekiah. It couldn't be him.

Shutting the door, I left and then stared at the meeting room.

Why had the light been on the day Liesel died?

As I was peering through the windows, Kodiak and Felicia came out of the filing room. They both looked a little disappointed.

Feeling at a loss, Cody sighed heavily. "We couldn't find anything."

I smiled sympathetically at my friends. "Thank you both—it's okay."

Giving me a sad smile in return, Felicia said, "Did you want to head back and see the whale exhibit now?"

I shook my head. "Go ahead without me, guys. I

think Grandmother and Rhys may have already left to see them. Meet me there in a few minutes?"

They nodded, agreeing though looking a little confused. We waved, and I watched as they exited the hallway.

Staring back into the meeting room, I sighed. Because no one was inside, I opened the door and flicked the light switch on.

What meeting was going on in here six years ago?

It felt that the clues were possibly clicking into place. Recalling our most recent discussion with Uriah Harper, I fell silent.

I need to think of motives.

There was no good reason that my father's income would have sunk. Either there was a miscommunication, there was some foul play, or both. Possible motives seemed to be either greed or perhaps jealousy—maybe even both. Was someone greedy or jealous of Dad, trying to get his money?

"Perhaps…" I whispered, "someone was after his job."

If Liesel's death was connected to Father's financial problems, though, then how did her passing factor into this?

I gazed around the meeting room, holding my breath. Surely the answer was in here somewhere.

"Wait," I muttered aloud to myself. "If the meeting was… Could it have been about *Father…?*"

It was all beginning to make sense. A drop in

income, workers quitting, and… a girl in the wrong place at the wrong time.

I gasped.

Was I getting ahead of myself? It seemed like I was onto something, but what if I was just grasping at straws… like I had done two years earlier?

Suddenly feeling uneasy, I slipped out of the meeting room, thinking of the potential dark business that could have taken place there years ago. Shutting the light off, I then closed the door.

Could Liesel Allen… have been killed to hide a secret—maybe a secret in the meeting room?

As I turned to walk out of the hall, I gasped, stunned into silence.

Staring at me was a man, standing not further than about seven feet from me.

"Oh, I-I didn't see you," I stuttered. "Sorry, I was just leaving."

The person in front of me was just the one I had been starting to suspect only about ten minutes earlier.

The man didn't move at all, and I realized I was trapped. Slowly, I backed away.

Everything seemed to click, but my mind was swimming with thoughts.

As I walked backward toward the filing room, the man started walking in the same direction.

"Sir," I nervously said, "if you'd just let me pass, I'll be on my way."

He was silent.

My eyes turned toward the meeting room at my side and then back toward him. In one smooth motion, I spun on my heel and ran down the hallway away from him, toward the filing room.

Technically, I needed to be running in the other direction, *toward* him, so that I could get out of here and back to the aquarium exhibits (where visitors like me ought to have been). Unfortunately, the hallway was narrow, though, and this man wasn't going to let me pass.

As I dashed through the filing room, I quickly snatched some folders and threw them toward the ground to cause him to trip and hinder his pursuit. I hurried to the end of the room and then sprinted to the backdoor. Thankfully, it wasn't locked. My heart thumping, I entered and slammed the door shut, now in the janitor closest.

It was dark in here, and I couldn't find the light switch, so I felt around the walls for the door to the other side, which would lead me to the reef tunnels.

What a relief it is that there are two ways out of the staff areas!

Finding the door at long last, I threw it open and ran out. My eyes beheld the magnificent creatures of the ocean, swimming above me and to my sides in the tunnels. I took a shaky breath, then ran with all my might through the room. Although *I* was busy today, to say the least, the aquarium as a whole wasn't, so people weren't in the tunnels. If only they had been! Then I could have called for help. As I

126

was running, I looked over my shoulder and saw *him* running out of the janitor's closet, coming toward me.

As a grown man, he was faster than a fourteen-year-old girl, and I knew it would only be a matter of moments before he would catch up with me.

There was a fork in the road, so to speak, as the tunnels split into two different sides. The left side would eventually lead to the jellyfish room's entrance while the right side would lead to a staircase. Running with all my might, I was nearly at the fork.

The staircase, which had a door at the top leading to the second floor, wasn't for visitors but was for the staff to take care of the sea creatures. The ginormous tanks containing the marine life didn't have a glass lid of any form on the top. It was open water and needed to be that way so the workers could care for the animals on the top story of the building. The area had a floor where the workers could walk around all the sides of the tanks and look down below at the animals.

I was about to turn to the left side of the tunnels so that I could reach the jellyfish room, but at this moment, the man caught up and pushed me.

I stumbled back and fell. Looking at him in horror, I was speechless.

"Get up," he hissed sharply. I did so, and he motioned for me to enter the tunnel on the right,

which would lead us to the staff's stairs. He was behind me, so I had to go where he wanted and couldn't escape.

After only a few minutes of brisk walking, we reached the stairs and I was forced to go up.

"Don't try anything," he said firmly, grabbing me by the arm and unlocking the door. He led me into the huge second floor.

On my left and also on my right appeared the open water from the tops of the tunnel tanks. For fear of falling in, I didn't dare walk anywhere but forward.

Struck with horror, I finally broke my silence when deep annoyance washed over me. I wanted answers and had had enough of this treatment. The man's grip was fierce, for one, and he was a monster!

My resentment far outweighed my fear.

I spun on my heel to face him. Voice loud from feeling so upset, I shouted, "Mr. *Bayer!* It was *you*, wasn't it? *You* were my father's assistant manager, and *you* were trying to get his job!"

Staring my oppressor straight in the face, I realized he was pale. Shouldn't I have been the one white with dread? No, I wasn't going down without a fight!

Narrowing my eyes at Zeb Bayer, I said, "But it didn't work, did it? Even after my parents died, you didn't get Dad's job; Mr. Colville did."

He was silent. Anger bubbled up inside my chest.

"You were talking in the meeting room, weren't you? You were talking to someone—who it was, I don't know—and one of you must have… Liesel went to unlock the doors and take some things to the filing room. She must have seen you and your accomplice in there. Mr. Zeb Bayer, would I be correct in assuming you were afraid she heard your meeting? The evidence needed to be covered, didn't it? So one of you—"

"Stop!" Zeb Bayer shouted, terrified and gripping tighter on my arm. "I didn't mean to kill her; it just happened!"

The next moment was a blur.

As soon as the words left Mr. Bayer's mouth, he shoved me with terrible strength. It would have been hard for anyone to stay on their feet with a push like that, and I lost my footing. Falling backward, I gasped—and plummeted into one of the reef tanks.

The chilly water was horrible. Tightly, I clenched my teeth. Because of the shock of it all, I couldn't think of anything for a moment. Still, what a relief this was an *aquarium,* and not an *ocean,* which would have been filled with untamed sea creatures. Even so, how was I going to get out? Actually, *could* I get out?

It seemed quite hopeless. My parents had died at an aquarium, and now… I felt a most horrible irony.

Perhaps I should have left things alone. Father and Mother wouldn't have wanted this.

My gaze fell on a starfish. Without a care in the

world, the animal silently relaxed on a rock.

Mother… your favorite creature.

I was sinking. All I could do was stare at the starfish, thinking of my family. I missed Mom terribly, and Father, too.

But my friends and my grandmother—they *needed* me. Didn't they?

Beginning to feel a little delirious from the lack of oxygen, I saw something above me but couldn't tell if it was real or just in my mind. Confused, I squinted a little and waved my arms up toward it, trying to reach.

I grasped whatever it was. The next thing I knew, I was being pulled out of the tank, coughing and gasping for breath.

As I coughed harshly, the scene before me was stunning. Ryker Nobleman and Uriah Harper were holding Zeb Bayer down on the ground! And Adam Bennet, who had just rescued me from the reefs, was now assisting them.

In an instant, Cody and Fay were kneeling next to me, both staring with utmost concern.

"Oh, *Lydia!*" Felicia breathed. "Do you feel all right? You've given us such a scare!"

Cody, nodding vigorously with a face looking anxious, said, "Lia! How long were you down there?"

"I-I don't"—I choked out and then coughed severely—"know for sure. Where's Grandmother?"

"She's getting help—calling the police," Felicia

quickly explained.

My hacking finally subsided after a bit, much to my relief as well as to my friends'.

"Why—when—how did Mr. Harper and Mr. Bennet get here?" I asked, shuddering and completely soaked from my unfortunate plunge. I wiped a wet, brown lock of hair from my eyes. We were a long way from Wilsonville, after all, so their appearance was certainly unexpected, to say the least.

"I have no idea," Cody said, "but I'm sure they'll fill us in on all of that soon enough. For now, let's get out of here."

Rising, we watched as the two adults, followed by Ryker, ushered Zeb Bayer out of the room.

I knew, at long last, that justice would be served.

Heavy and Light

Chapter 10

A blanket of snow lay across the ground, and the bare branches of the trees pointed up toward the crisp sky. The weather was still frosty, but the season was losing some of its strength with the passing of days. Soon, everything would be blooming and bursting forth with life again.

As the cold winds blew, a strawberry-blond teen ran down the sidewalk, laughing with glee.

I laughed too. Exchanging glances with Felicia, we hurried after our best friend.

Only two and a half months had passed since we

did this same thing, prior to becoming part of a mystery, but it felt like ages.

"Hurry, Fay!" I shouted enthusiastically. "We've got to catch up to Cody!"

"Oh, Lia," she replied with uncertainty, cautious as she looked at the slick sidewalk. "I don't want to slip."

I knew my best friend had a valid point. She called out to Kodiak, pleading that he'd be careful, but I wasn't sure he heard. Eventually, though, we all arrived at Cody's house, and with no bones broken.

Since the events of our visit to the aquarium and, to put it mildly, my unfortunate dip into the coral reef, two weeks had passed.

Zeb Bayer confessed to his crimes. While he had been Father's assistant manager at the aquarium, he was discontent with the position, wanting more power. Mr. Bayer had then tried to cause strife in the aquarium, spreading rumors and getting people to quit in hopes of the owner viewing his manager, Seth Arlington, as the problem. He was so sly that he even got the owner of the aquarium's faith in my father to waver a bit. The boss began to dock Dad's pay. While Zeb's plan did seem to be effective as my father began losing income, Father's job was given to Hezekiah Colville after his death. What a surprise for Mr. Bayer! Interestingly, the boss didn't feel that

Zeb was truly the right man for the job, so Mr. Bayer's scheme was only effective in part. If only Father's boss had realized all the reasons that Zeb didn't deserve the position.

Zeb had an accomplice, however, who was discussing plans with him on the morning that Liesel entered Scottsbluff Aquatic Museum. The accomplice had since quit the job, likely feeling miserable working in the place that held his dark past, and moved to a different part of Nebraska. Because authorities tracked him down, he would clearly be getting questioned before long.

On the morning of Liesel's death, the two men had been in Father's office, trying to find things to use against him before entering the meeting room. Blaire Forbes and Liesel Allen had driven to the aquarium earlier than usual, making their arrival unexpected. Upon seeing Miss Allen, Zeb and his accomplice feared she had heard their plans and would give them away. So in the heat of the moment, Mr. Bayer extinguished his suspicions in the worst kind of way. Yet, all he gained from his actions was much *more* fear and a miserable conscience.

Liesel's death was to hide a secret—one concerning my own father.

Clearly, all of this was a powerful example of the wickedness of greed and jealousy. If Zeb Bayer

would have just addressed the issues of his heart from the beginning, he would have never found himself in the meeting room on that day, and Miss Allen would likely still be alive.

Unfortunately, people's bad behaviors don't always affect just them, but others too.

Stomping to get the snow off his western boots, Cody arrived at his backdoor. "Come on, girls, what's the fun of competition if I always beat you anyway?"

"Kodiak," said Fay, "how about a match of chess, then?"

Most of Cody's face paled, but his cheeks blushed.

"Well?" Felicia inquired, smirking a little.

I laughed. "Oh, Code, I believe it's only fair that if you race us, you'd better play chess with Fay, too."

As the three of us walked inside the Nobleman house, I could tell my strawberry-blond friend was searching for a way out of this trap. However, at a loss, he smiled and agreed to inevitably lose to Felicia.

"I hope you enjoy the victory, Fay," said Cody while he slipped off his boots and then greeted Felicia's three-year-old sister, Leanne.

"Don't speak like that, Kodiak," Fay responded with a snicker, shaking her head at the boy. "If you

assume you can't win, you won't. If you assume you *might* win, who knows?"

In the kitchen, Mrs. Nobleman, Mrs. Blackwood, and Grandmother were chatting and preparing dinner. A cozy smell of baked blueberries filled the room. Immediately, my friends recognized the scent and the recipe.

It was at this this moment, Ryker came skittering down the stairs, exclaiming just what his brother and Fay were thinking: "Midnight blueberry crunch!"

"I didn't know you and your grandma were bringing that," Cody said to me, suddenly looking very hungry. "But I doubt anyone will spare us a slice until after dinner. Guess I'll have to grab a snickerdoodle, then!"

He left to do so, and Fay and I burst into a fit of giggles.

Coming toward us, Ryker said, "Unless my eyes deceive me, it looks like we've got two giggling schoolgirls here."

The teen then proceeded to take his reading glasses off and rub the bridge of his nose. He squinted at us for a moment.

"Nope. My eyes and ears haven't tricked me at all," he said. Then, he observed the baking dish of blueberry crunch, which had just been taken out of the oven. "And my *nose* hasn't, either."

Returning with his snickerdoodle, Cody said,

"Lydia, I asked your grandmother why she calls her recipe midnight blueberry crunch. I was hoping it wasn't because we have to wait until midnight to eat it."

Amused, I inquired, "What answer did Grandmother give you?"

"Well, first she explained that *you* made it today, Lia. Second, she answered that it'll have everyone *up* at midnight, wanting the snack."

Feeling honored by my grandma's kind words, I blushed a little.

Ryker replied that he'd be happy to put Grandmother's statement to the test. Cody agreed, finishing his snickerdoodle.

"Also," Fay said, "it appears we're having some grilled peppers with dinner tonight. That's what Mrs. Nobleman told me."

Smirking, Ryker and Cody exchanged glances.

"They'll be too hot for you, Cross Eyes."

"Will not!"

Fay and I playfully rolled our eyes at the brothers.

While the four of us were chatting, the doorbell rang, so Mrs. Nobleman called out to her sons to let the guests in.

As they did so, three men and two women entered. It looked like we'd have a full house this evening.

"Hi, Uriah!" Cody chirped. "Hello, Nicole; hello, Gracelynn; hello, Adam; hello, Miles!"

The next moments were full of greeting and talking and laughing. I was glad to see Uriah conversing with Nicole and her sister, Gracelynn. Exchanging glances with Fay, I smiled slyly at my friend. A feeling of joy was rising in my heart.

"Oh, Lia," Felicia breathed in a whisper to me, "do you think we'll have a *wedding* to attend in the future?"

"Well, Fay," I began, looking at our detective friend and his sweetheart, "by the looks of it, I'd say we have a pretty good chance."

Felicia went to help Cody set up the chessboard, and Ryker was preparing to watch their long, intense match. Kodiak really wanted to prove himself.

"How've you been, Lydia?" I heard from behind me.

Spinning on my heel, I saw who spoke and beamed.

"Thanks to you, Mr. Bennet, I'm alive and well!"

Slightly embarrassed by the compliment, Adam let out a small laugh. "Don't mention it. I… only wish I could have helped your parents five years ago…"

Letting out a soft sigh, I nodded. "I know you would have done whatever you could. If it weren't for your help, I'd be drowned. Truly, I'm positive

my parents would be forever grateful to you for saving my life from that reef exhibit."

A teen cleared his throat. "I may not be your family, but *I* for one am grateful. You gave us a pretty horrible scare there, Lia."

"Oh, Ryker," I said, "I gave *myself* a scare."

He shuddered upon recalling and then said, "But, Miss Allen's family finally got the closure they never had thanks to you."

"Oh no," I said, "not just me. If it weren't for the rest of you guys, Zeb would still be getting away with murder. Each of us played a part in solving the case."

"It was a crazy, crazy ride," Ryker agreed. He looked as if he wanted to continue the discussion but was then cut off by Cody, who was waving his hands wildly in the air, motioning for us to come. "Cross Eyes and Fay have the chess game set up," Ryker concluded. "Want to watch?"

I laughed, my heart feeling a strange mixture of heavy and light. "I wouldn't miss it for the world."

While I followed Rhys to the living room, Adam Bennet went to socialize with his close friend, Uriah.

Turning to me, Ryker gave a slightly concerned, somewhat teasing smirk and then said, "When you're an investigator again, don't fall into any more aquarium tanks, okay?"

"What do you mean about investigating again?" I

asked, my lips curling into a small smirk.

He laughed. "Knowing you, I've got a feeling this won't be the last case you'll want to solve."

Deep down, I realized Ryker was right. Lately, I was feeling this… pull… to help those who were hurting—to bring justice. Although it's horrible, heart-wrenching things do happen, and the world can be pretty dark. Someone needs to bring a light.

"Your move, Kodiak."

Felicia's words yanked me from my deep musings. Taking a seat on the floor near my friends, I observed Cody's careful, pondering face. He reached for one of the chess pieces on his side of the board, then paused before lifting a different pawn instead.

"Hey, Miles, want to join us?" Ryker asked, looking at the young man who was chatting with Fay's father. "And you too, Mr. Blackwood! Your daughter's going to beat Cross Eyes again."

"She is not!" Cody exclaimed. As the words left his mouth, however, Felicia proceeded to grab one of her pieces, a knight, and skillfully capture Cody's queen.

"Pitchfork!" the strawberry-blond teen wailed.

Ryker held up his hands in defense. "It's not my fault you didn't guard your pieces better."

Cody shook his head in disappointment. "Don't distract me anymore, you rascal."

140

Intrigued, Mr. Blackwood and Miles Carpenter approached to see the game. Soon, it wasn't long before everyone was watching. Even Mrs. Nobleman, Mrs. Blackwood, and Grandmother had temporarily abandoned their cooking.

Every burden that had weighed down on me from the beginning of our adventure to the end seemed distant. Although part of my heart still longed for my old life, I began to truly embrace the new, and I recalled my parents with fond memories rather than sadness. With thanksgiving, I silently acknowledged just how much God blessed me with.

"Fay!"

Kodiak Nobleman's exclamation showed he lost—yet again. But even still, he truly seemed to be having fun.

You'll get the hang of it, Cody, I thought. *Eventually.*

Surrounded by so many loved ones, all was at peace.

ABOUT THE AUTHOR

DANIELLE RENEE WALLACE is a teenage author
born in Washington State. She established a large
love for reading during her elementary school years
and a strong love for writing while in middle school.
At fourteen, Danielle published her first book, while
living in Lubbock, Texas. Her father spent about one
year of his boyhood in Wilsonville, Nebraska, the
town in which Danielle's series, *Secrets of the
Abandoned Bus,* takes place. Currently, she resides
in northern Ohio with her parents and two older
brothers.

Scottsbluff Aquatic Museum

backdoor

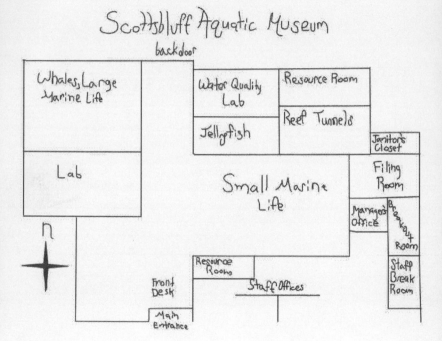

Whales, Large Marine Life

Lab

Water Quality Lab

Jellyfish

Resource Room

Reef Tunnels

Small Marine Life

Janitor's Closet

Filing Room

Manager's Office

Breakout Room

Staff Break Room

n

Resource Rooms

Front Desk

Staff Offices

Main Entrance

THE
CASE OF 1999

DANIELLE RENEE WALLACE